TOBY

TOBY

by **Marc Talbert**

*Dial Books
for Young Readers*

New York

Published by Dial Books for Young Readers
A Division of NAL Penguin Inc.
2 Park Avenue, New York, New York 10016

Published simultaneously in Canada
by Fitzhenry & Whiteside Limited, Toronto
Copyright © 1987 by Marc Talbert
All rights reserved
Designed by Nancy R. Leo
Printed in U. S. A.
COBE
1 2 3 4 5 6 7 8 9 10

Library of Congress Cataloging in Publication Data
Talbert, Marc, 1953–   Toby.
Summary: Toby, the child of a "slow" father and
a brain-damaged mother, uses his very normal ten-year-old
wits to survive peer pranks and adult do-gooders
who want him placed in a foster home.
I. Title.
PZ7.T14145To 1987   [Fic]   87-5333
ISBN 0-8037-0441-0

In celebration of
Willard and Ellen Talbert, David and Moy Williams,
Mary and Sam Long, and Ollie Canvin.

TOBY

1

Toby was in the dusty dark, under the front porch with his dog, Whiskers, curled up quiet and listening to the rain. At the approaching slap of shoes on the puddled sidewalk, his body tensed and he lifted his head. The porch steps groaned as the shoes stomped and then strode across the porch to the front door.

Each time a shoe landed, the floor above Toby glowed as light slipped through gaps between the sagging boards. Each patch of light disappeared and then reappeared a couple of feet closer to the door, off to one side or the other—right, left, right, left. Toby followed the glowing steps, squinting at them through his eyelashes.

Toby knew whose feet filled those shoes. The boards sagged like that whenever Reverend Olsen walked across the porch.

But Toby felt safe under the porch. Nobody ever looked for him there. He figured that most people were afraid that black, hairy spiders would drop from the darkness and bite their necks or crawl under their shirts. Or they must be afraid that spiderwebs would gum up their eyelashes, gluing them together. Or, Toby thought, they must be afraid of touching shriveled, leathery, diseased varmints that crawl under porches to die. Or they must be afraid of centipedes skittering over their legs or grubs popping gooey and crunchy every time they put down their hands or knees.

People being afraid of going under the porch—that was fine with Toby. To be alone, he went under the porch. Just himself and Whiskers. He'd cleaned out most of the bugs and dead things. Sometimes spiderwebs would be stretched across the darkness if he hadn't been there for a while. And once he evicted a skunk, chunking mothballs under the porch as though they were grenades.

Sometimes, when Toby was under the porch, he curled up, closed his eyes, and pretended he was inside his mother—before he was born. Like now. Curled up, Toby wondered if the wind swooshing and the rain falling on the grass and the sidewalk and the house sounded like his mother's blood when it swished around and around him before he was born. And he wondered if her heart sounded like the *da-thud, da-thud, da-thud* of the footsteps walking above him. Her bones must have rubbed together at the joints and creaked when she moved, like the screen door opening. And his mother's voice must have been muffled through her chest like the faint, slurred voice coming through the floorboards right now.

"Rev'ran Ol-sin. Calm in."

Sometimes Toby wished that he'd never been born.

"Thank you, Mary . . . er, Mrs. Thurston. I'll only be a minute."

A minute. That's a bunch of chickenfeed, Toby thought. Especially since he's here because of me. I know what's coming next, he thought, stretching out like a baby being born. He jammed his elbow into the powdery dirt and propped his head in his hand.

"Mrs. Thurston, is Toby here?"

"No." Toby's mother's voice was flat and strained. Toby cringed. She sounded retarded. But she's not, Toby thought, clenching his teeth. She's not, she's not, she's not . . . retarded.

Toby's mother was like the dented can of peaches he had picked out of the bargain basket at the grocery store and that now sat on top of the refrigerator for tonight's dessert. In high school his mother had been in an accident and her skull got mushed. Caved in. Dented. Her brain was hurt. Her words were crippled and slow. The peaches in that can are still sweet, Toby thought, drawing his name in the dirt with his poking finger. And so is Mom's brain. She loves me, Toby thought, mashing his name with his fist. And she loves Dad.

"I see." Reverend Olsen always talked to Toby's mother slowly and loudly—as if talking louder helped her understand better. He talked loudly to Toby also. "Well, Toby ran away from school today. Mrs. Gunderson asked me to come see if Toby was here."

Toby pictured Mrs. Gunderson, the principal at his school, with wisps of hair coming undone from her old-fashioned bun, her heavy cheeks lifting and falling when she talked, like pulled curtains moving in a breeze.

Whiskers sneezed and licked Toby's face. Toby put his arm around the dog and pulled her closer. She licked his face again—on the lips. Toby didn't mind.

"Wha' hop-panned?"

Mom doesn't need to ask, Toby thought. Reverend Olsen will tell her anyway.

"Harold told me that Toby just flipped out and started . . . Well, let me put it this way: He urinated on Harold and then ran away."

Harold was Reverend Olsen's only child. Whatever Harold told his father, his father believed. It was like the song that they sang in church every Christmas—the one that went "Hark, the Harold Angel sings." Reverend Olsen believed his son was an angel.

But Toby knew Harold wasn't an angel. Harold loved to pick on Toby. Because of that, Toby stayed away from Harold as much as he could, especially now that Harold thought he was in love. Unfortunately, staying away from Harold wasn't easy. Like today.

Harold had picked a bad time to fall in love. A couple of weeks ago, Toby and Harold's fifth grade class began studying "Human Growth and Development." That was Miss Follensby's way of not having to say "sex." All the girls tried not to snigger when Miss Follensby said *penis* out loud—which she did seventeen times in two weeks—everybody counted—and the boys would try not to smirk. And the boys would look at their desk tops when Miss Follensby said *vagina*—which she did thirteen times—and the girls would try not to blush.

Miss Follensby acted as if nobody had any feelings when she said *penis* and *vagina*. Toby thought that was stupid. Everybody *knows* that boys walk around with penises, he told Whiskers one day under the porch. He could feel his, scrunched up in his too-small jeans. And every girl has a vagina. And *everybody* has breasts that are pretty much the same in fifth grade—except for Robin, who'd just moved from New Jersey. You just don't *say* so, he explained to Whiskers after the first day. It's embarrassing.

Whiskers had thumped her tail in agreement.

The kids in Toby's class tried to act cool anyway, but Toby noticed that they started to look at each other sideways—as if they were trying to figure out what everybody else looked like under the sags and wrinkles and bulges of their clothes. And they acted as though they were afraid people could see through their clothes. That made everybody weird. Especially Harold, who was crazy about Robin but didn't know how he should act around her anymore.

That's when Harold and some of the boys started

drawing dirty words and pictures of naked girls and boys on the partitions between the toilets in the boy's room. They signed everything they drew with Toby's name.

Yesterday Miss Follensby took the boys to a corner of the library and talked with them about vandalism and about how sex wasn't a dirty thing but something wonderful between two people who loved each other. Even though Toby's name was all over the partitions, she looked at Harold while she talked. Harold fixed a hurt look in his blue angel eyes. But several times Harold's eyes flashed angrily when he stole glances at Toby. Miss Follensby noticed.

This morning the partitions in the boys' room were gone. Miss Follensby explained that they'd been taken down for refinishing because of all the graffiti on them. She said that she hoped that would be a lesson to all the boys who had vandalized school property.

Toby avoided going to the bathroom as long as he could. He hated the idea of sitting on a toilet or standing in front of the urinal in the middle of a big, tiled room, without privacy, afraid that somebody would walk in at any time—just when he farted or grunted. He crossed his legs. He unbuttoned the top button of his jeans. He scooched down into his chair to give his bladder more room. He tried to hold on until noon, when he planned to rush out to the edge of the playground and pee behind a bush.

But when he felt as if he would pop, Toby asked for permission to go to the boys' room.

He was standing in front of the only urinal in the bathroom, nervously trying to unzip his jeans before anybody came in, when a first-grader burst into the bathroom. Startled, Toby looked over his shoulder and saw the little boy running and pushing his pants down at the same time. The kid's face was puckered in concentration and he stopped behind Toby, dancing on one foot and then the other, his pants and underpants banding his knees together, his eyes pleading for Toby to finish. Toby turned back to face the wall and closed his eyes. Come on, come on, he encouraged himself. Come on.

Toby heard a stream of water hit the urinal. Surprised, he looked down and then over his shoulder. The kid was aimed between Toby's legs, peeing as if he were putting out a fire.

"What're you doing? Why didn't you use a toilet?" Toby didn't move, afraid that the kid would hit one of his legs.

"Big boys use this thing," the kid replied, pulling his pants up hurriedly and scurrying toward the door at the same time. The door flew open and bumped the kid backward, sitting, onto the cold bathroom floor.

"Watch where you're going, punk," Harold said, glaring down and holding the door open. The kid scrambled to his feet and, rubbing his shoulder, charged out the door, his head lowered.

Harold looked up. "Well," he said. "Look who's here. The class pee-brain."

Toby felt a shrinking below and turned back to the wall. He gritted his teeth.

"The class retard," Harold said, taking a few steps toward Toby. "Re-tard, re-tred, re-tred, re-turd," he taunted.

Toby tried not to flinch. He closed his eyes and felt himself relax below.

"I'm surprised you even found your little thing-y."

Toby blushed. He better leave me alone, he thought. He better leave me alone.

"Maybe you don't even have one," Harold said, sniggering.

Toby opened his eyes a crack. "Wanna bet," he said, turning his head and looking at Harold through his eyelashes.

"Yeah," said Harold, smiling. He crossed his arms over his chest and rocked back on his heels.

Toby's heart pounded. This is it, he thought. As quickly as he could, Toby whipped around and sprayed toward Harold, aiming for his face. He'd never aimed up before and missed. Instead, Toby hit the shoulder and arm of Harold's shirt. Harold gasped. "Yuck!" he yelled, hopping out of the way. Toby turned to follow him. He hit Harold right above his pants.

Harold was backing away as Toby ran out of ammunition. Before he could stuff himself back in, Toby charged out the door, down the hall, out the building, and across the playground. He raced down the street, darted into the gully behind the Lutheran church, and charged into the woods. He stopped for a minute to catch his breath and do himself up. He held his breath and listened. Nobody had followed him.

Victory and fear fluttered in his chest. Toby jammed his hands into his pockets and walked slowly back to his house, being careful that he wasn't seen. As always, Whiskers was waiting for him. Together they snuck around the porch and crawled under it.

Toby heard Reverend Olsen's voice above him, soaking through the porch boards. "That was very immature behavior for a child of his age. It just isn't normal. We must begin to face the facts that Toby may be . . . disturbed. This certainly isn't the first time he's done something this immature. And it's been happening more frequently lately. . . ."

Who wants to be normal? Toby thought. Harold's supposed to be normal—and he smelled like pee until his father came to school, picked him up, and took him home.

2

The rain stopped, but large drops splattered onto the sidewalk from the trees, sounding to Toby like worm-eaten apples hitting cement. The wind breathed halt-ingly, like a person after a hard cry. A car sloshed by.

"Thange kew, Rev'ran Ol-sin." Toby listened as his mother walked Reverend Olsen to the front door—her steps uneven, his firm and predictable. "Thange kew."

"We're all one family in God's eyes," Reverend Ol-sen said. "And family should take care of family. Good-bye."

You can tell a lot about people by the way they walk, Toby thought. Reverend Olsen tromped across the porch and down the stairs. The boards creaked, shaking the porch, and Toby shuddered. He half expected a shiny black, rubber-heeled shoe to splinter through and land on his face. Toby closed his eyes and pictured Reverend Olsen walking down the sidewalk, his neck stiff in a starched clerical collar, never bending to look at his feet—but never tripping or stumbling.

The sound of Reverend Olsen's footsteps melted into the sounds of spring—the cricket chirp, the beat of frogs, the bird song. The air tossed and turned, sighed, and comfortably rearranged itself. The leaves rustled and sent shivers of raindrops onto the sidewalk.

Soon after Reverend Olsen's footsteps disappeared, Toby heard the sound of other shoes biting into the driveway along the side of his house. The shoes stopped, a car door ground open, and springs squeaked as somebody threw his rear into the seat. The door slammed shut, sounding to Toby like a metal lid slamming onto a metal garbage can. The car exploded to life and tires kissed concrete as the car roared out of the driveway, its anger fading like the light outside.

Mr. Bertram is nasty, Toby thought. I hate him. And he hates me. He thinks Whiskers piddles on his bushes and digs up his weedy-looking flowers. He calls me a retard. Toby shut his eyes tight and pictured Mr. Bertram—a short, dumpy man, almost as wide as he was tall, with thin ankles and tiny feet. His belly poked out from under T-shirts showing his big, yawning belly button. Mr. Bertram chewed slowly on gooey cigars and aimed his thick, brown spit at Whiskers every chance he got. He's just like his car, Toby thought—old, slow, loud, smelly, and dripping oil.

Toby sighed. Through the powdery air he smelled dampness from rain that had seeped under the porch from the sidewalk and grass. Worms, he thought. Tomorrow I'll have to be careful of worms, coated with dirt flour, wriggling painfully under the porch.

Toby rolled over onto his hands and knees. I wish I were a big, black cat, Toby thought. I'd sharpen my claws on Mr. Bertram's anklebone.

He raised his rear into the air like a cat's tail, squinted his eyes into angry cat eyes, and hissed softly into Whiskers's face. Whiskers lifted her head and licked Toby's nostrils. Toby hissed again, louder, and playfully struck out at Whiskers's shoulder with clawed fingers.

Whiskers turned her head to one side and sniffed toward her tail. Slowly, she rolled over and her legs splayed apart. Her upper lip fell away from her mouth and Toby saw her white teeth in the shadows.

Toby tried one more time—dipping his head down until his chin almost touched the dirt and hissing into Whiskers's ear. Unimpressed, Whiskers licked Toby's chin and sniffed at the wet spot she'd made.

"Oh, all right," Toby sighed, sitting back on his heels. He reached over and scratched Whiskers's tummy. "Let's go see ol' lady Bertram."

Toby liked Mr. Bertram's mother as much as he disliked Mr. Bertram. Either Mr. Bertram had never married or his wife had left him and taken the kids—Toby wasn't sure which. But Toby knew that Mr. Bertram lived in the house where he grew up, with his mother. Instead of having a wife, Mr. Bertram had his mother to cook and clean for him until last Christmas, when she'd had a stroke. The stroke slowed Mrs. Bertram down for a couple of months. But she seemed fine now—except that she believed that she was dead.

Mrs. Bertram may think she's dead, Toby thought as he crawled out from under the porch. But she's nice.

Toby knocked at the kitchen door and waited. He heard steps approach but the door didn't open. Whiskers's tail thumped on the step in anticipation. Toby reached out to knock again. The door flew open and Mrs. Bertram's wrinkled face popped out.

"Boo!" she said, her cheeks flapping out and falling back. She stared, as if in a trance, over the top of Toby's head.

Toby studied her. She was wearing a huge green bathrobe that probably belonged to her son. She had three long white hairs sticking out from her chin. Her nose was narrow and delicate, barely separating coal-black eyes that glowed fiery when she was angry. She had no eyebrows and her thinning white hair stood straight up, as if she were looking at a ghost.

"Hello, Mrs. Bertram," Toby said, smiling. The first time she greeted him that way, he'd been too surprised to be scared. His lack of fear had satisfied her that he was a ghost boy come to call. She told him that she didn't want to deal with nasty little boys if they weren't ghosts. "Live boys give me a headache," she'd said.

"Come on in, there," she said, opening the door with a creaking that echoed her own voice. Toby reached for the door and held it open for Whiskers, who hesitated a moment before walking in, her tail limp. "You know you don't have to knock. Silly little boy ghosty. You should just walk on through the door." She turned and, with quick light steps, scurried to the sink. "Just makin' some bug juice," she said, grabbing the counter and looking over her shoulder, smiling. "Want some?"

He nodded and watched her clutch a juice container and, with both hands, tip it, sloshing purple juice into one jelly glass and then another.

"Even the dead got to keep their strength up," she said, holding a glass in each hand and walking quickly to the living room. The juice bucked and lapped at the rim of each glass, spilling over in dribbles. Toby and Whiskers followed in her wake.

"Have a seat," she commanded, handing him a glass. Standing with her back to a chair, she held her glass with a straight arm and level with her waist. She dropped backward, keeping the glass exactly where it was, now level with her chest. "Ah," she said, winking at the undisturbed juice. "Here's to restin' in peace," she said, grinning at Toby. Tipping her head back, she swallowed the juice with a glugging sound. She set the glass on the arm of the chair. A purple mustache stained her upper lip. "What's good for the body is good for the soul," she said.

"Yes," he said, smiling at her and taking a sip of

juice. His nose pinched together as fumes rose from the back of his throat and into his sinuses. Just like last time, she'd spiked the juice with gin.

"It shore is nice not to be caught up in the worries of the living," Mrs. Bertram said. "The living are so stupid sometimes I just wan' ta shak' 'em. And I would, too, if I weren't passed on. Why, I got a letter today from my niece in Florida askin' me to come on down fer a visit. A visit!" Mrs. Bertram lifted her hand to slap her knee and her elbow knocked the juice glass off the chair. It clattered as it rolled on the wooden floor. "Can you imagine askin' a woman what's dead down fer a visit?" she laughed, dropping her hand to her lap. "Poor, poor addle-brained Francine. If only she knew what a relief it is to be dead. Why, if she knew she'd jump in front of a train in a minute!" Mrs. Bertram chuckled.

Toby nodded. He pretended to take another sip of the juice and then set it down on the floor at his feet. Whiskers's tail thumped and she lifted her head to sniff the glass. Her tail dropped to the floor and she quickly drew her head from the glass. Whiskers laid her head on her paws and gazed at Toby, disapproval dulling her eyes.

The first time he'd visited Mrs. Bertram after her stroke, Toby wondered if she wasn't just pretending that she was dead to scare him. But each time he visited with her, the more he thought she truly believed it herself.

"What kind of silliness did you see today . . . out

there?" She nodded toward the living room's front window.

"Well," Toby said, getting his thoughts together. He scratched an itch on his thigh through his jeans. "I saw some bully tormenting a littler kid in the bathroom at school. Thought he could get away with it too. But you know"—he studied Mrs. Bertram and decided to say it anyway—"the little kid just turned around and hosed down the bully but good!" He was relieved to watch Mrs. Bertram's eyes widen and her mouth drop. She whooped and stamped her feet.

"I'll jes' bet that cooled off the bully a tad!" Tears leaked out of the corners of her eyes and she brushed them away. "Now ain't that the limit. And that little squirt jus' hosed 'im down. Little squirt, nothin' . . . *big* squirt!" And she whooped again at her own joke.

Toby smiled. "That's right." He hesitated. He didn't tell jokes often—only if he could screw up his courage. He gulped air. "And you could call that bully Harold a pee-head now!" he blurted.

"Pee-head!" Mrs. Bertram shrieked so loudly that Toby was afraid somebody outside would hear and rush in to help. Suddenly her mouth clamped shut and the smile disappeared from her face. "Harold, ya say?" Toby nodded. "Why, I knew a Harold when I was a kid. Had a stink like a cornered skunk and a personality to match. But I had a likin' fer the critter. Handsome boy. And he knew it too." She squinted at Toby, who nodded.

"Fact is, I used ta spy on ol' Harold. Follow 'im

wherever he went. Couldn't stand ta keep him outta sight. Why one afternoon—musta been in August or thereabouts—a hot day, mind you, where your clothes just stick like they was glued to ya—I followed Harold and a bunch a boys to a swimmin' hole. Didn't let 'em know I was there, 'cept ever once in a while my brother Tad would look back spookish like he heard me, only he didn't. He was jes' scared Momma was on his tail 'cause he'd gone without her say-so."

Toby watched Mrs. Bertram's face relax, dreamy, and she tilted her head back slightly and closed her eyes. "Well, I knew it was wrong. But I hid in a bush and watched those boys snake off their clothes. They jumped around and around bare naked and as white as ghosts 'cept fer their faces and arms. They was frolickin' and laughin' and drunk on the danger a being caught thatta way. Why it was a sight for a young girl to behold, and educational too. Ever' one of 'em was built jes' like my brother Tad, know what I mean, and I was relieved to see Tad was at least normal in this one respect."

She sighed. "Well, that Harold jumped in right away and scared the fish all the way ta the next county. The others stood around, shiverin' and shakin', daring each other ta get in while he called 'em chicken livers and momma's boys and worse. Finally, Harold came outta the water, drippin' sheets, and crawled up into a tree leanin' out over the water. Standing there, white as a marble statue in the sun after a rain, and jes' as shameless, he told 'em boys standin' on shore that he was gonna spit a glob into the river below and if they didn't jump into the water on top a his spit he was goin' ta take their clothes, fill 'em with rocks, and dump 'em in the middle of the river."

Toby leaned forward, wanting to know what happened next.

"And you know what?" Mrs. Bertram asked, looking down at him and smiling. "Ever' one of them boys jumped on a glob a ol' Harold's spit! And when I cheered after the last one, you never saw such a surprised look on ol' Harold's face. Why, he being the only one stuck out on a limb without a stitch on, I thought he was gonna bust out and cry." She grabbed both arms of her chair, her elbows pointed back like wings, and pushed down with a grunt. Steadying herself, she walked toward the kitchen. "Some things jes' don't change, and a bully's one of 'em." The words floated over her shoulder like a trailing scarf. "Want some more bug juice?" she called.

Toby looked out the window and saw that darkness was falling.

"No thanks," he said, standing up. He and Whiskers walked into the kitchen. He watched Mrs. Bertram pour herself another glass. "But thanks anyhow."

"If our parents only knew. Why I wouldn't a walked straight fer a month or more." Mrs. Bertram didn't say good-bye. She just kept talking as if he had always been with her and never left. "It is such a blessin' to be passed on. . . ." he heard her say as he quietly closed the kitchen door and eased the screen door back in place.

He jammed his hands into his jean pockets and looked down at Whiskers, who was looking up at him. "She's nice, Whiskers," he said quietly. "Even if she does drink bug juice."

The clouds were moving fast. They were boiling and breaking in the west. The setting sun made them blush in patches and glow in stripes.

The air smelled washed, like breathing through a clean, wet sheet hanging on the line. The birds hushed as the sun sank slowly behind the Bertrams' house. Toby held his breath as the red glow of the sun made their roof look afire. He watched as the clouds drained of color, looking like smoke rising from the roof. The clouds darkened and stars popped out. The clouds rushed on, like a tattered velvet curtain being drawn open across the night sky.

Toby turned toward his house. Every light was on. He walked up the sidewalk and turned to face the front door. He bowed his head against the light, as if it were a wind, hoping that he wasn't in trouble about what happened earlier in the day.

He looked up and saw his father's shape framed in the screen door. He couldn't tell if his father was smiling or frowning. But Toby smiled bravely into the light as he climbed the stairs, knowing that his father could see his face and hoping that a smile would soften his father's mood if he was angry.

"Toby," his father said, pushing the screen door open and letting the boy and dog inside, "we were gettin' worried. Whare you been?" The screen door slammed shut.

"Talkin' to Mrs. Bertram," Toby said, studying his father's tired face. "Just talkin'."

His father's face broke into a smile and his eyes shone proudly. Toby breathed out, relieved. "You wasn't jes' diggin' up ol' man Bertram's flowers now, were ya?" his father asked, talking as if his tongue were too big for his mouth.

"Naw," Toby said, grinning. "Did that last week."

"Ah, you," his father said, cuffing Toby lightly on the side of the head. "Git worshed up. Dinner's ready." He reached an arm around Toby's shoulder and drew him in for a one-armed hug. Toby smelled the slaughterhouse on his father's work shirt—blood and the sourness of guts. When he came home from work, his father washed to get rid of that smell. But the washing made a sickly sweet combination of soap perfume and blood smells.

Toby ducked and broke away from his father's arm. "Yore jes' too smart fer me." His father chuckled, watching Toby scamper away.

Toby burst into his parents' bedroom, the only one in the house. He made a beeline for the house's only bathroom, which was attached to the far end of the bedroom like a lean-to shed. Even their bedroom smells a little like the slaughterhouse, Toby thought as he turned on the water.

Toby's school was right next to the slaughterhouse. He held a finger in the water, waiting for it to get warm, and watched the water run over his finger in a band and fall like a ribbon toward the drain. He avoided looking at the face in the toothpaste-spotted mirror above the sink and thought about the smells and sounds that drifted into the classroom from the slaughter-house. First thing in the morning, just before the bell, came squeals as pigs were unloaded from trucks and into holding pens. As they sat doing math, the squeals died down as pigs were subtracted, one by one, from the rest. The quiet of reading was disturbed by the faint odor of blood and then the stronger stench of burning hair as the pigs were killed and drained and shaved and the hair burned. After lunch, the smells were more complicated, like the smell of ham itself, as the meat was chopped and processed and cooked and packaged.

Toby reached for the soap and lathered up his hands. He ran his hands through the water and ran them through his hair, matting down a cowlick that always stuck up toward the back of his head. When he was little he pretended the cowlick was a feather and that he was an Indian. Sometimes he still pretended.

Toby looked at his parents' bed as he walked to the living room. He'd loved to sleep cuddled up between his parents when he was small. Now he slept on the pullout couch—or he snuck under the porch when the weather was good and he felt like it.

"Whooee," his father said as Toby walked into the kitchen. His father was standing with his arm around his mother's waist. His mother was buttering toast on the counter. "You look clean enough ta be bran' new!"

Toby grinned as his father walked to the stove and lifted a saucepan from the burner. Toby smelled canned spaghetti. Whiskers followed Toby's father from the stove, keeping an eye on the pan. As Toby's father dished out the spaghetti, Whiskers sat at his feet patiently waiting for dabs of food to fall on the floor.

Toby's mother shuffled to the table with her plate of toast and smiled at Toby. He looked at her hopefully, not knowing if she'd told his father about Reverend Olsen, but figuring by now she hadn't.

"Hep your mother," his father said, setting the pan near the place where he always sat. Toby walked over and helped his mother into her chair.

"Now, tell me 'bout school," his father said as Toby sat down. "You doin' okay in yore figgers?"

Toby looked up at his mother and smiled. She smiled back. She hadn't told on him and Toby's stomach yawned in relief.

3

Toby ran all the way home from school. He'd put a piece of white bread from lunch into a back pocket of his jeans and sat on it all afternoon. Now it was pressed thin as a slice of luncheon meat and he wanted to give Whiskers this treat so badly he felt like bursting.

Whiskers sat up from her place on the porch as Toby charged up the sidewalk to his house. She shook herself as though she were wet and dropped her shoulders to stretch her front legs, yawning at the same time. She watched Toby disappear around the corner of the porch and, sedate as a lady negotiating church stairs after Easter services, walked off the porch, around and through the lilac bush, into the familiar darkness where Toby sat grinning.

"Looky what I got for you," Toby said. He arched his back to lift his rear from the dirt, balancing himself with one hand while he reached into the back pocket of his jeans with his other hand. He eased the bread from his pocket, careful not to tear it. He sat back down and folded the leathery, white square once. "Here." He held out the pale triangle in his hand.

Whiskers sniffed at it, daintily took a long corner in her tiny front teeth, and pulled it off Toby's hand. With a grunt, she sat and then lowered herself onto her elbows, laying the bread across her paws like a napkin.

"Go on," Toby whispered excitedly. "Eat it!"

Whiskers sniffed it again and the bread disappeared in two chomps. She sniffed her paws for crumbs where it had lain.

"How was that?" Toby asked, reaching over to her and stroking the ridge of her nose. Her tail swished over the dirt.

Above him, through the floorboards, Toby heard the babble of a TV game show his mother was watching. A man's voice was excitedly describing some things behind curtain number four. His mother often watched that show, waiting for his father to come home. Instead of waiting on the couch with her, Toby settled down to wait for his father beneath the porch. His mother still hadn't told his father about the other day at school. And Toby knew she never would. But

Toby was afraid that without his father around his mother would ask questions: Why did he pee on Harold? How was he doing in school? Did he have any friends? Was his teacher nice?

Sitting in the dark, Toby pictured his mother straining to ask those questions, her mouth and lips and tongue not cooperating with each other. The hurt of being unable to talk would knot her forehead and make her fingers kink and writhe. Her eyes would show the panic of being trapped inside a body that didn't work right and of thoughts and feelings trying to escape a brain that jumbled and confused them.

How could I answer her? Toby wondered, picking a burr from Whiskers's fur, pulling a tuft of hair with it.

I don't know. That would be his answer. And his mother would deflate like an old balloon—wrinkled, with her lips flapping.

Toby heard steps turn up their sidewalk. Each of his father's steps lingered a moment before the next one, the toes of each foot getting a good grip before they pushed forward. Toby tipped his head up as his father climbed the stairs and walked across the porch. The boards didn't groan and his father's footsteps didn't glow like Reverend Olsen's—not even a little.

Whiskers's tail thumped happily in the dark. Toby closed his eyes and saw his father with a big grin stretched across his face sneaking up to his mother. Toby pictured his father lifting into a sore-footed tiptoe and, when he was right behind her, reaching his hands around each side of her head and covering her eyes.

"Guess who!" Toby heard his father say, laughter thickening his voice.

"You!" his mother blurted.

"How did you know!" His father laughed.

Toby heard air whoosh breathlessly from the couch cushions as his father plopped next to his mother. They never get tired of that routine—like two-year-olds throwing a ball back and forth and back and forth and back and forth, Toby thought.

Toby turned toward Whiskers. "Ready?" he whispered. Her tail thumped faster. He rolled onto his hands and knees, crawled to the edge of the porch, and peered out from behind the lilac bushes. Whiskers was right behind, sniffing the bottoms of his sneakers.

Toby didn't see anybody. He crawled out another foot or so and quickly stood up. He bent down to brush dirt off the knees of his jeans and then walked around the porch, up the steps, and through the front door.

From behind, his parents looked like two bodies attached to one head. His father was kissing his mother, his arm around her shoulders. Toby stopped. He tried to turn around quietly and leave. Instead he tripped on a shoelace and sprawled on the floor at Whiskers's feet.

Toby scrambled to his feet and sheepishly watched his parents untangle themselves and turn in the couch to look back at him. His palms stung from sliding across the floor and he rubbed them together.

"Well, well." His father smiled, his arm falling from

his mother's shoulders and dangling down the back of the couch. "Caught us a-kissin'."

His mother blushed and she tried to frown. But her smile was too strong and the combination smile and frown made her look as if she were going to cry.

"T-To-bee," she stammered, the blue of her eyes straining at the corners of her eyes so that she could see him. "Better git worshed up." She gulped air. "Yer gran-pair-ants is a-comin'."

"Ya." His father's smile faded. "They's takin' us out ta Bishop's ta eat." By the tone of his father's voice Toby knew which grandparents were coming. Toby nodded glumly and walked past his parents, toward the bathroom. He thought of all the wonderful food at Bishop's that he could eat—ham and potato salad and Jell-O with tiny marshmallows and chocolate silk pie. And he knew that he wouldn't enjoy any of it because his mother's parents would watch him like a hawk and criticize the way he wiped his mouth and sat in his chair and how big his bites were and how he sometimes hummed when he ate his favorite foods.

Toby watched Whiskers drink from the toilet bowl as he washed his hands. His grandmother had caught him trying to drink like that when he was small. Toby cringed, remembering the spanking he'd gotten. That was the first memory he had of his mother's parents. Since they retired and moved to Des Moines they didn't visit often, even though they were only a couple hours away. But when they came it always meant trouble was brewing. Nobody had told him in so many words, but Toby knew that his mother's parents didn't like their daughter to be married to his father. And they don't like me either, Toby thought.

Toby wiped his hands dry on Whiskers's back, running one hand all the way up her tail. He grabbed a hunk of toilet paper to wipe off the water spots Whiskers had dribbled onto the toilet seat. He dropped the damp paper into the stormy patch of water and returned to the living room to wait on the couch with his parents. The television was off but his parents stared at it anyway, lost in their own thoughts. Next to him Toby's father became more and more tense. As the minutes crept by, the couch twitched as his father nervously bounced the heel of one foot up and down and up and down on the floor.

The three of them stood when they heard a car pull up in front of the house. Toby glanced up at his father's troubled face. He reached over and grabbed his rough hand and squeezed it. His father looked down at him, worry melting away from his eyes for a moment, but returning when he looked up again toward the front door.

Toby's grandmother stood in the doorway and crossed her arms in front of her. Her purse dangled from the crook of her arm, swaying as gently as the loose pouch of skin hanging above her elbow. She walked into the room and looked down at Toby as if he were a stain on the rug. "How are you doing, Toby?" she asked, her critical eyes as cold as her steel-gray hair.

"Fine," Toby said, as he always did.

Her mouth stretched thin in disbelief.

Toby's grandfather came in, taking off his hat. His shoulders were rounded and his jacket hung loosely on his wiry frame. His chin stuck out, just like Toby's mother's did when she was concentrating. "Sit down, sit down," his grandfather said, as if he were the host instead of the guest. He waved his hand up and down impatiently. Whiskers sat at Toby's feet, looking up at Toby's grandfather, her tail still and her ears alert. "We invited Reverend Olsen and his family to join us. He'll be along in a few minutes."

Toby reached down to feel one of Whiskers's ears. I hope Harold made up a good excuse not to come, Toby thought.

Toby's grandmother surveyed the room looking for a place to sit. Toby's father studied her for a moment, wringing his hands, looking like a little boy too embarrassed to ask where the bathroom is. His face suddenly lit up and he grabbed a chair sitting against the wall next to him. He brought the chair over to his mother-in-law and tried to help her sit. Instead, he banged the chair against the back of her knees. Her legs folded and Toby's grandmother sat with a grunt and a look of scorn instead of thanks.

Toby's mother sat back down on the couch and her father sat at the other end from her, staring vacantly around the room in every direction but Toby's. Toby and his father remained standing.

Nobody said anything. Whiskers began to pant softly.

Toby's grandfather cleared his throat a couple of times and Toby watched him fiddle with his wedding ring, twisting the gold around and around his finger. His grandmother opened her purse and felt around inside it, peering. She pulled out a wadded tissue, closed her purse with a snap, and tucked the tissue between her wrist and watchband.

A car stopped in front of the house, its engine idling. With groans and wheezes, Toby's mother struggled to her feet, ignoring her father's offer of help and they all walked out of the house. Toby looked back at Whiskers before he closed the door behind him. "We'll be back," Toby said, closing the door.

Toby sat between his parents in the back of his grandparents' car. Silently, they followed Reverend Olsen. Toby looked between the dashboard and the rearview mirror at the three heads in the car in front of them. With his short hair, Reverend Olsen's head looked like a peeled egg with a flat dent on top. His wife's head was twice as large and lopsided because of her hair. Toby squinted and shifted his head to one side so that the box of tissues sitting on his grandparents' dashboard hid Harold's head.

Toby avoided Harold by closely following his grandmother as she pushed her tray down the runners of the buffet line.

"I know I shouldn't be eating this, but it looks too good," she announced, pulling a plate of onion rings from under the sneeze guard—and two rolls with four pats of butter, a fruit salad held together with whipped cream, a large pickle sitting in its own little plate, roast beef with potatoes and thick, brown gravy, and creamed corn. When her tray was filled, she turned to Toby and said, "Here, take this for me." Toby put the lemon meringue pie next to his red Jell-O with marshmallows.

Toby filled his own tray so full that the edge of his plate with ham and cherry sauce cut into a sweet potato sitting on the next plate, and the plate of chocolate silk pie barely balanced between the lemon meringue and the Jell-O with marshmallows. He pushed his tray carefully toward the cash register, where his grandfather stood, billfold in his hand, waiting to pay for everybody.

"Sure you can eat two desserts?" his grandfather asked.

"One is for Grandmother," Toby said.

His grandfather nodded. "Well then you won't mind if I put it on my tray, will you?" He pulled the plate of lemon meringue off Toby's plate.

"Let me help you with that, sonny." A young man in a brown Bishop's uniform walked up to Toby. He took Toby's tray from him and walked ahead toward the table where everybody else sat.

The young man pulled out a chair next to Toby's grandmother and opposite Harold. Toby looked wistfully at his parents at the other end of the table. "Enjoy your meal," the young man said and walked away.

"Toby, where is my pie?" His grandmother turned from Reverend Olsen and scowled at the plates in front of Toby.

"Grandpa has it," Toby said, looking at Harold.

"I hope so," his grandmother said, "or . . ." She turned back to Reverend Olsen. "Now what was I saying? Oh, yes. Des Moines isn't so bad but . . ."

Harold kept staring at him, a smile twitching at the corners of his mouth. Toby looked back down at his food. Nothing looked as good now as it had when he chose it.

"Hello, Toby." Harold's voice was mockingly polite.

Toby looked up. Harold took a bite of his drumstick and chewed slowly. Toby looked back down at his food. He didn't feel hungry at all.

"Do you need help cutting up your meat?" Harold asked in his angel voice.

Toby swung his leg out and watched Harold's face twitch as his foot connected with Harold's shin. "I guess you don't." Harold grimaced.

"How are you boys doing?" Reverend Olsen leaned over the table and looked around Toby's grandmother. He winked at Harold and Toby noticed a dab of mashed potato on Reverend Olsen's chin.

"Fine," Harold said, smiling back. "We're doing just fine. It was nice of you to invite us, Mr. Clay." He looked along his shoulder to Toby's grandfather and smiled broadly.

"Glad you could come," Toby's grandfather replied. He turned to look at Harold and studied him for a moment. "You know, you look an awful lot like your granddaddy—the one you're named after."

"That's nice," Harold said, his smile shrinking.

"Ol' Harold and I used to pal around a little. What a pistol that bugger was. I could spend a month of Sundays tellin' you the trouble we used to get into."

Toby reached for his fork and cut off a piece of ham. The saltiness tasted good and he began to feel hungry.

"That would be nice, sir," Harold said doubtfully.

"Why one Halloween we turned over every outhouse in the entire town and moved every one of Mrs. Henry's sleeping chickens into her best parlor without waking a chicken . . . or Mrs. Henry."

Toby's grandfather nodded and smiled. "And we used to pick on a little runt—brother of a neighbor of yours, Patsy Bertram—what was his name?"

"Tad," Toby said without thinking.

His grandfather looked at him with surprised eyes. "Yes, his name was Tad." He closed his mouth and squinted. "How did you know?"

"I visit Mrs. Bertram sometimes." Toby looked down at his plate of food and wished he were a ghost and could disappear. He could feel his grandfather's inquiring eyes roaming around his face.

"Samuel, must you talk about such things at the dinner table?" All eyes turned to Toby's grandmother. "You don't need to go putting ideas into young boys' heads. This'n," she said, nodding toward Toby, "has a good enough imagination for trouble as it is." She put down her fork. "Toby, your napkin is meant to be used."

Toby raised his napkin to his mouth. He pretended to use it and twisted his mouth into a snarl instead.

"Just tellin' Harold here how much he reminds me of his granddad. Sweet as pie to the grownups. Mean as a momma bear to us kids. Never could trust 'im when he was a kid, even when we were friends."

"Dad had a mean streak in him," Reverend Olsen said, nodding. "Luckily, he didn't pass that on to our Harold."

Harold smiled sweetly at his father and aimed a kick that hit Toby right below the kneecap.

They drove back in silence. Toby's stomach was as full as his head. He hadn't said another word to Harold at dinner and hadn't looked up from his plate until he'd finished eating everything. The air in the car was stale and smelled of onion and coffee breath. Toby felt the lump in his jean pocket to make sure Whiskers's treat was still there. He'd wrapped a ham rind up in a napkin and he hoped it wasn't leaking juice onto his jeans.

Darkness was falling as they pulled up to their house. Toby waited for his mother to hoist herself out of the car. He gave her a little push from behind and she turned to smile at him as he followed her. The doors of the Olsen car popped open and Reverend Olsen, his wife, and Harold got out.

"Come in and set a spell," called Toby's grandfather.

"Just for a minute," Mrs. Olsen called back.

"You and Toby go play somewhere," Reverend Olsen said to Harold. He turned to Toby. "And be on your best behavior."

Toby and Harold watched as the adults walked up the sidewalk and inside the plain-faced house—eye windows on either side of a door nose that sat above a thin-lipped porch and a long ribbon of sidewalk tongue. Whiskers bounded out the door like a sneeze as the house filled to overflowing with light, which spilled out the windows and onto the lawn. She came up to Toby, ignoring Harold, her whole body wagging.

"You know," Harold said, taking a step toward Toby and folding both arms on his chest. "I haven't had a chance to talk to you about the other day. In the bathroom." A sly smile crept across his face. "You really pissed me off, you know?"

Whiskers's body stopped wagging and she looked up at Harold, her ears folding flat against her head. Harold looked down at Whiskers and the smile disappeared for a moment. He took a step back.

When he looked up at Toby his eyes were glittering. He unfolded his arms and jammed his fists into his pants pockets. "I just want you to know that you'd better watch out. I'll get you. And I'm going to take my time, too. You're going to get it worse than our grandpas used to do to that Tad Bertram."

Toby's heart pulsed and his head throbbed. "Yeah?" he said through his teeth.

"Yeah." Harold took a fist out of his pocket. He examined his knuckles. "I don't like the way you look," he said, "or the way your whole retarded family looks. I hate you," he said, coolly looking up at Toby. "I wish you and your family were dead. You're all my dad ever talks about. You know what my dad said the other day? He said that you should be taken away from your parents. And you know what else he said? He said *we* should take you in! He said it would be the Christian thing to do. And it would be easy because I never cause them trouble."

Harold turned his back to Toby. "You can go and play, Mr. Re-turd," Harold said. "I'm going home."

Toby and Whiskers watched Harold walk across their lawn and down the street. *Live with Harold?* The thought of that made the ham he'd eaten start crawling up his throat. When Harold was out of sight he and Whiskers slipped around and under the porch.

His head buzzed from what Harold said. Toby lay on his side, punched his elbow into the dirt, and propped his head on his hand. He tried to breathe deeply. Whiskers lay down alongside him, her nose sniffing at the pocket that held the ham rind.

The voices that he heard through the floorboards sounded like they came from an old-fashioned radio. The floor and furniture creaks and pops sounded like radio static crackling.

"I don't know why we should have to worry about such things at our age," he heard his grandmother grumble. "We should be taken care of by our children and grandchildren, not the other way around. If only we'd been more careful, Reverend Olsen, things wouldn't be so bad. We insisted that Paul have an operation . . . whatchama call it . . ."

"Vasectomy," his grandfather muttered.

"Yes," continued his grandmother, "and we thought that would keep them from having children. Don't believe we haven't thought of suing that clown who thinks he's a doctor."

"Now, now," Toby heard Reverend Olsen say, "the good Lord put Toby here on earth for a purpose. Sometimes that . . . sometimes pregnancy happens after a vasectomy. We can't second-guess the Lord."

"The smartest, strongest little fishie got through, I'll warrant," he heard his grandfather say. "We're lucky for that. And we're lucky to have you to look after our little Toby, Reverend Olsen."

Toby's hands shook and his head quaked on its arm pedestal. He lowered his arm, resting his head on his shoulder, and hugged Whiskers closer to him. They had studied vasectomies in school last week as part of "Human Growth and Development." He remembered Miss Follensby telling the class that it was a way of not having babies—a way where a man's tubes, the ones coming from his testicles, are tied or cut. He could see Miss Follensby now, explaining it to them. She taped two drawings on the chalkboard—one of a man's insides and one of a woman's. As she said the name of each body part she pointed it out on one drawing or the other. About vasectomies she'd said: "It keeps sperm from passing into the woman, swimming up her fallopian tubes, and fertilizing her eggs."

Embarrassed yet fascinated, Toby remembered those words. Sperm were tadpole-like things that came from the little, egg-shaped testicles he could feel between his own legs. And the eggs came from ovaries deep inside women. He knew that when a sperm and egg married, a baby grew inside—safe and warm and protected.

So they had tried to keep his father's sperm away from his mother's eggs. They had tried to keep him from ever being born. The thought was strange and frightening and Toby shuddered.

"He is getting older and harder to manage every day," Toby heard Mrs. Olsen say. "You may want to consider a foster home for him." Toby held his breath and listened harder. Harold had been right.

"Maybe here and maybe in another town," Reverend Olsen continued. "Toby needs help from somebody who understands him. But he may also need to be someplace where he could get a fresh start. Harold tells me that the kids tease Toby something terrible but every time he tries to help, Toby strikes out at him— tries to hurt him or get him in trouble."

"I don't much care for charity," Toby heard his grandfather say. "Maybe we could take him in. Des Moines is a big place. We should be able to find some kind of help for him there."

"I'm just too old and too tired to look after a little bag of mischief," his grandmother replied. "Look. All our lives we've worked hard—and it hasn't been easy. We've suffered through more than our fair share of bad luck and unhappiness. We should be taking it easy, enjoying ourselves a little while we can. I just won't have Toby living with us. Why, you saw the way he was at the table. He eats like a horse, or like that dog of his."

"No." Whiskers's head jerked up at the sound of Toby's mother's voice. "To-bee is our boy. He b-longs here—wi' us."

"We don't have to make any decisions tonight," Reverend Olsen sighed. The floorboards complained as he stood up. "But we should all be thinking about this."

"Thanks for the dinner, Mr. Clay." Toby heard Mrs. Olsen stand. "We better get home now, honey. I have a million things to do."

"We should be headed for home too," Toby heard his grandfather say. "Don't much like to drive in the dark."

The house shook as everybody walked to the door.

"Nigh'," he heard his mother say.

"Harold! Toby!" Reverend Olsen called. "Harold! We're leaving!" He paused for a moment and heard nothing. "Har-old!"

"Don't disturb the neighborhood, dear." Mrs. Olsen's voice was sharp. More gently she said, "Just tell him to come on home when he and Toby get back from playing."

"Okay," Toby heard his father say.

The door closed. His parents didn't move and Toby pictured them holding each other tight—like he was holding Whiskers—to keep from shaking.

4

Miss Follensby called them family trees. For the past half hour all the kids in the class had been busy drawing grand, dignified, oaklike trees on pieces of manila paper that covered their desk tops. Miss Follensby had told them that each large branch was to be named for some important ancestor and the smaller branches were for living relatives.

Toby craned his neck to look over Robin's shoulder. He saw that her family tree was large and oaklike, so thick with names that the letters looked like leaves. Robin's busy pencil stopped in the middle of a name and her shoulder tipped his way.

Toby fell back into his seat and hunched over his desk. Peering through the curtain of hair that fell over his eyes Toby stared at Robin's back. She reached over her shoulder with the eraser tip of her pencil and dug into her shirt, underneath her bra strap. She pulled back her shoulder blades and leaned over the back of her desk chair. In a flash, Robin whipped the pencil out from under her strap and the pencil slashed the air in an arc, missing Toby's forehead by several inches.

Just as quickly, Toby reached out as if he were swatting a fly and snatched the pencil from her hand. Robin's shoulder tensed and Toby dropped the pencil over the edge of his desk. It bounced once on its eraser and clattered down the aisle, stopping at Robin's feet.

Robin glanced back at him as she leaned over to pick it up, a frown wrestling with a smile. Toby covered his smile with the back of his hand, pleased with himself, and looked down at his blank piece of paper.

He tried to picture his own family tree. He nibbled on the lead point of his pencil, tasting a sweet saltiness, and wondered what Harold's tree was like.

If Toby held his head a few inches from his desk top and turned it to the right, as if he were listening to his piece of paper whisper, he could see Harold's tree. Harold's tree was lopsided, as if somebody had pruned every branch off the left side. It looked like the trees along the railroad track. Every spring, men standing on a slow-moving flatbed railroad car chopped off new growth that might bang into the trains as they barreled down the track.

A hand touched Toby's shoulder and he jumped and jackknifed at the same time. His knees smacked the bottom of his desk, smarting, and the desk's edge dug into his stomach. He looked over his left shoulder. Miss Follensby was frowning.

"Why, Toby." Miss Follensby's voice was too quiet. "I didn't know your paper could talk." She took her hand off his shoulder and leaned toward him. Her lips pulled together like the mouth of a drawstring bag. "You did ask your parents about your family tree last night, as I asked?" She spoke slowly and distinctly, as she might to a second-grader.

He hadn't asked. His parents went to bed soon after his grandparents left last night. And Toby snuck in after the house was quiet.

But Toby nodded, staring down at his paper, his lips retreating into his mouth.

"Good." Miss Follensby drew herself up until she stood straight and tall and thin as a young willow. "Please start drawing. We don't have much time before science."

She walked down the row of desks, her hands behind her back and tied together with long, thin fingers. She looked back and forth, right and left, observing the family trees growing on every desk top.

If I don't know my family tree I'll make one up, Toby decided. Miss Follensby will never know the difference. Toby drew a straight line just above the bottom of his paper. On top of this line he drew the base of his tree—thick, branching into two large limbs, close to the ground. One side for my mother and one side for my father, he thought.

Toby's heart started pounding as he remembered what he'd overheard last night. Toby wrote his mother's parents' last name—Clay—on the lower branch on the left side. He piled on top of that name other names that popped into his head—Smith, Brown, Ford, Chevy.

Near the top and on the right, just below Whiskers's name, he wrote his father's parents' name—Thurston. He liked those grandparents. They still farmed a couple of counties away. In the summer they sometimes took Toby to their farm for a week at a time. Toby loved the farm. He and Whiskers would help round up the mild cow, Margaret, and last summer Toby learned to milk her. All the animals, except the momma pig, were friendly. Even the cats brushed up against Whiskers's legs, purring and their tails straight up. And every fall, just before school started, his father's parents sent Toby money to use for buying new clothes and school supplies.

Below them, Toby filled in the other branches with names he remembered from books—Charlotte and Wilbur, Peter Pan and Wendy, Max, and St. George.

Miss Follensby probably won't like this, he thought. But she will probably believe me if I tell her these people are the ones my parents told me about.

Toby nibbled on the end of his pencil, squeaking the wet eraser against his teeth, and looked at his tree. If he were a man pruning trees on the railroad, he knew what side he would chop off.

Out of the corner of his eye, he saw Harold's foot shoot out sideways from his desk and back again—as fast as a snake tongue flicking. A triangular pillow of folded paper skidded next to Pete's desk, two seats in front of Toby. Accidentally-on-purpose, Pete dropped his pencil onto the floor so that it landed next to the triangle of paper. He bent sideways to pick up the pencil and palmed the paper at the same time. Passing notes this way is so obvious, Toby thought. And Miss Follensby hardly ever catches one.

Toby watched Pete pretend to scratch the back of his neck. The note dropped quietly onto Robin's desk. Robin's hand shot out to cover it. Sheltering it in her palm, she glanced at it and, just like Pete, scratched the back of her neck. Toby followed the note with his eyes as it fell, covering THURSTON on the manila paper. He read TOBY printed on the top so that, together, the letters were shaped like the triangular piece of paper. Toby flipped it on its back, as if it were a round-backed bug. Like little bug legs, squiggly lines formed the word RETARD.

Toby stared at the note for a moment. The paper was folded tightly, but Toby was careful not to tear it along the creases. It was as hard as undoing a double knot in his shoelaces. Toby frowned as he spread the crinkled paper with his hand. What he saw looked like the drawings on the partitions in the boy's bathroom. In the middle of the paper was a stick figure labeled TOBY. Standing over this figure was a bigger stick figure with a smoldering cigarette hanging out of the corner of its smiling mouth. A lasso-like bubble came from the big figure's mouth confining the words "Time to change your diapers?"

Toby slowly wadded the paper into a tight ball, careful not to make any sound. He popped the wad into his mouth and let his saliva soften it. He chewed slowly, pushing the pasty-tasting wad around his mouth with his tongue.

Toby looked at Miss Follensby, who was in the front of the classroom writing vocabulary words on the chalkboard for science. Her dress swished back and forth as her arm moved up and down.

Toby reached into his mouth with his thumb and pointing finger and gingerly pulled out the pulpy wad. Holding his other hand under the wad to keep it from dripping onto his family tree, Toby took careful aim and tossed the spitball toward Harold's head. He watched it land on the back of Harold's neck with a satisfying smack as soft as a sloppy kiss. The wad slid down the collar of Harold's shirt and out of sight.

Harold sat up straight and arched his back. Toby imagined the wad falling, leaving a wet streak down Harold's spine and lying trapped above the small of his back where his shirt tucked into his pants. He watched Harold pull out his shirttail and nudge the spitball over the edge of his pants and onto the floor behind his chair.

Toby looked at his paper and pretended to put some finishing touches on his family tree. Out of the corner of his eye, he saw Harold look back at him, disgust and anger competing for space on his face. Toby drew a cloud in the sky above the tree. He closed his eyes and imagined himself lying on his back on top of the cloud, his face to the sun, floating out of the picture altogether.

"Okay, class." Toby's eyes flew open. "Time to hand in your family trees. Robin and" —she looked around the room— "John, would you pick up the papers and put them on my desk?"

Robin turned around in her seat and looked Toby in the eye. "Boy, are you going to get it after school," she whispered, not moving her lips. She put her paper on top of his and picked them both up. Toby looked at her through his eyelashes and smiled. He heard admiration in her voice and saw laughter in her eyes.

The bell rang. Toby watched the class pour out the classroom door, heads bobbing like water rushing down a pebble-strewn gutter and into a grate. Toby stood up slowly and walked toward the door. Instead of turning left and outside, he turned toward the library.

Mrs. Windish thought Toby was very thoughtful to help her so often after school. Toby liked Mrs. Windish and he didn't mind shelving books for her—it was better than being beat up by Harold.

"Am I glad you're here!" Mrs. Windish said, as Toby walked into the bright openness of the library. "I've got a million books to put away and I haven't been able to do one all day." Toby pushed a cart piled with books toward the stacks in the back of the room.

"Look out for books that have been put in the wrong

place," Mrs. Windish called. "Somebody has been de-
liberately mixing up the books on the shelves. I can't
imagine who."

As he shelved books, Toby played a little game with
himself. He tried to guess who had read each book he
picked up and then looked inside the cover to see if he
was right. He guessed right that Robin had read *Are
You There God? It's Me, Margaret.* But he was surprised to see Harold's name directly under Robin's.

Toby was just looking inside *Island of the Blue Dol-
phins* when Mrs. Windish walked up behind him. "I'm
going to take off, Toby. I need to take my daughter to
the dentist. You'll have to leave."

Toby parted two other O'Dell books and stuck the
book between them. "Okay," he said.

"I could give you a ride home," Mrs. Windish said,
cocking her head to one side.

"That's okay," Toby replied. "I'll walk."

Toby thought Mrs. Windish was nice to ask. But he
would have been uncomfortable riding in her car all by
himself. And he didn't want Harold to see him and think
he was afraid to walk home.

"Suit yourself," Mrs. Windish said, turning and
walking away. "Maybe next time. Thanks for your
help."

Toby charged toward the door that led from the wing
with the first and second grade classrooms. He grabbed
the panic bar and pushed as he ran, not breaking his
stride. Without looking around, Toby scurried around

the corner of the building and ran across the street toward the railroad tracks.

"There he is!" Toby heard somebody shout behind him. A stampede of footsteps followed.

Toby raced down the tracks and ducked into the thicket of trees. He crouched, like a scared rabbit, gasping quietly. His eyes widened as he heard the crunch of footsteps on the cinder bed of the tracks. He froze, not breathing, and his ears pricked up like Whiskers's when she heard her name.

"I don't believe it!" he heard Harold explode. "We lost that little retard again. Where does he go?" And Toby heard Harold kick out and cinders ping against the steel rails. "He could be anywhere—up that hill or over toward that house. Damn." Harold's voice grew louder.

"We'll get him next time." Toby heard Pete's softer voice.

"And we'll make him hurt twice as bad as we would have this time." John's voice cracked on the last word.

"Yeah," Harold muttered. "You hear that?" he exploded, shouting. "You hear that, you re-turd?"

Toby's head shrunk deeper into his shirt, like a turtle. The crunch of cinders grew louder.

"Got a smoke?" Harold asked, sounding tired.

"Yeah," John said. "Here."

The crunching stopped. Toby heard a match strike. "That's better," Harold sighed. Toby whiffed smoke.

"Maybe if you didn't smoke you could catch him," Pete said.

"Who asked you, wussy," Harold said. "Just 'cause you get sick every time you try one."

Toby peered through the leaves and watched Harold, Pete, and John saunter by, trailing a cloud of smoke. When the crunch of their footsteps slowly disappeared, he crawled out of the bramble, stiff from his tense stillness. He looked up the track where he'd heard them go. The twin rails curved to the left and disappeared—empty.

Toby's heart slowed. He crawled out of the bushes and trudged toward the path that led to the back of the Lutheran church. He thought of Whiskers waiting for him at home. He pictured the porch and how quiet and dark and nice it would be underneath—as quiet and peaceful as he wanted the inside of his head to be.

Normally the darkness under the porch calmed Toby, hiding him from the confusion outside. But today, the darkness crowded him—causing thoughts to press around him, thoughts as unsettled as the fine dirt stirred up into the air when he and Whiskers crawled under the porch.

Someday Harold will catch me, Toby thought. And then what will I do?

Toby scratched around Whiskers's ears. She started to pant quietly. If he could see through the dark, Toby knew he would see Whiskers's eyes closed and the tip of her tongue cradled in her bottom fangs and delicately drooping from her mouth like a pink iris petal.

When she panted, her mouth drew up into a smile exposing her yellow-rimmed back teeth.

When he comes for me, Toby thought, I want to be tough. Tough and strong and mean.

Toby breathed deeply. His chest puffed out and he held his breath. I'll laugh in his face, he thought, listening to his heart beat faster and louder. And I'll put my fists on my hips and toss my head back and look straight down my nose at him. I'll stare him right in the eye. And I'll tell him that he's nothing but a bully and that I don't want to get my hands dirty by touching him but that I'll slap him silly if I have to.

Toby pressed his lips tightly against each other and jammed his tongue against the roof of his mouth to keep air from escaping. Air slowly leaked from his nose, anyway, sighing like a punctured tire.

Toby let out a ragged breath and his brave thoughts sagged like his chest. He shook his head. When the time comes I'll shrink like a worm crawling back into its hole, he thought. I'll close my eyes and run. And when I'm cornered I'll look at him through my eyelashes and try not to show him that I'm scared. I'll look at him and hope that he punches me someplace besides my face.

Whiskers's cold, wet nose touched his cheek and snuffed. Her tongue flicked out and dabbed him next to his mouth. "Aw, come on," Toby whispered, shying from her. "Don't get mushy." Whiskers licked his ear and put her head back on her paws.

Toby rubbed his ear dry on the round of his shoulder. What would *you* do, Whiskers? he asked silently, moving down her neck to scratch under her collar. What would you do if Harold came after you? Whiskers stopped panting and stretched her neck to make Toby's job easier.

Whiskers wasn't a fighting dog. Other dogs sensed that and just sniffed around her head and tail and left her alone. She hardly ever bared her teeth on purpose. Whenever he and Whiskers drove with his father's parents out to their farm, Whiskers stuck her head and chest out a car window and closed her eyes to slits and pulled her ears down flat. The wind would lift the flap of her upper lip and bare her teeth. Drops of water would fly back from her tearing nose and watering mouth onto Toby's face as he held her hind legs tightly, afraid that she'd fly out of the car when they hit bumps and potholes. Toby would look at Whiskers's snarling face and feel her tail squished against his chest and trying to wag, happy and excited.

That's the way Toby wanted to look when Harold caught up with him. But he knew that if he did look fierce, it would be an accident—like Whiskers with her head stuck out the car window.

Whiskers laid her head on the ground and rolled over onto her back. "Silly." Toby grinned and scratched her tummy.

5

Toby heard familiar footsteps coming down the Bertrams' driveway. He pictured Mr. Bertram landing on the balls of his feet, leaning backward but only lightly touching his heels to the ground. His belly would bounce and his straining T-shirt would ride up higher and higher with each step. The car door scraped open and the car groaned as Mr. Bertram threw himself into the driver's seat. The door crashed shut, the engine roared, and the car rattled away.

Suddenly, Toby wanted more than anything to visit Mrs. Bertram—to tell her what was on his mind, see if she had any advice from when she was alive.

"Come on," Toby whispered, patting Whiskers's belly. He felt Whiskers twist around and stand with a grunt and a fart. The smell of sour dog food filled the space under the porch. "Ugh," Toby muttered, trying not to breathe in.

Outside, the air was sweet and the wind coaxed the stiffness from the lilac branches. Whiskers was right behind him as he walked to the Bertrams' back door. He knocked on the screen door. He heard footsteps clatter across the kitchen floor and fade to silence. He knocked again and waited.

After a moment he heard a faraway, singsong voice from inside the house. "Come in," it called.

Toby pulled the screen door toward him and pushed open the kitchen door a crack. "Hello?" he called.

"Come in," came the faint, creaky reply.

Toby pushed the door just enough to slip inside. He held it for Whiskers. Whiskers looked up, her eyes searching his face and her tail still and limp. "Come on," Toby coaxed. He opened the door wider. "Come on." Reluctantly Whiskers took three steps and sat just inside the door. Toby pushed Whiskers's tail out of the way and eased the door shut.

The house seemed to be holding its breath—like Toby. But Toby noticed steam rising from the hot dishwater in the kitchen sink. A mound of soap bubbles poked over the edge of the sink like a shy cloud trying to hide.

What kind of a game is she playing now? Toby wondered, walking quickly through the kitchen and into the living room. The curtains were drawn and all the lamps were off in the dark, shadowy room. Toby looked over his shoulder toward the kitchen, his ears tuned for any sound. Whiskers hadn't followed him into the living room and the air felt spooky.

"Oh pshaw." Toby jumped and turned in midair toward the picture window. A frazzled head appeared from behind the sofa, faintly glowing pink in the curtain-flavored light like a tuft of fiberglass house insulation. "It's jes' you." Mrs. Bertram stood up and skirted around the sofa to stand in front of him. "Never know when you'll come a-poppin' in fer a visit, ghosty boy." She reached up and scratched the top of her head. In the watery light her hand reminded Toby of a chicken foot.

"Hello," Toby said, breathing in with relief. "How are you, Mrs. Bertram?"

"Fine as can be expected under the circumstances," she said, scurrying toward her chair. She turned and fell backward into its arms. "Feelin' no pain, which is a blessin' to those of us what led a difficult life." She squinted up at Toby. "Sit down, boy, sit down. Where's yer ghosty dog?"

Toby sat in the chair opposite hers. "In the kitchen," he said.

"Ain't doin' the dishes now, is she?" Mrs. Bertram cackled at her joke.

Toby smiled. She may be crazy, he thought, but I sure like her. He heard the click of Whiskers's toenails on the linoleum as she walked across the kitchen and stood waiting at the kitchen door. "Come on," Toby called softly, patting his thigh. Looking first at Mrs. Bertram and then at Toby, Whiskers walked around the living room, as far from Mrs. Bertram as she could, and sat next to Toby's chair.

"Ya know," Mrs. Bertram said, leaning forward and propping her elbows on the arms of the chair, "been havin' the strangest visions lately." She paused and studied Toby, her chin jutting forward with its long hairs glowing in the dim light. "The other night I imagined that I was alive again! Alive and bound to this earth and responsible for that lazy, good-fer-nothin' son a mine." She flopped back into her chair, her legs popping out and then settling down again. "I wuz jes' wonderin' if'n that ever happens ta you."

"Well," Toby began, not knowing what to say. "Well, sure." He squeezed his knees together and tried to think of something. "Like just the other day I had the strangest feelin' I was being chased by some boys, down the railroad tracks and behind the church."

Mrs. Bertram's back stiffened and she leveled her eyes on him. "I'm glad you've had the same experience. Why, my feelin' alive jes' about threw me fer a loop. I thought to myself, I said, 'Lookee, nobody lives forever,' I says. So I says, 'Maybe nobody dies forever either. Maybe,' I says, 'after livin' there's death and then life and then death and on and on until forever.'" Mrs. Bertram shook her head. "It gives me a headache ta think about it. I like bein' dead."

She clasped her hands in front of her and leaned into

the bridge her arms made. "An' if that weren't enough, I've been havin' some strange things happen to me lately. Seems that bein' a ghost, I jes' can't do nothin' 'bout 'em, neither. Makes me feel mighty helpless."

Toby watched her face shorten and lengthen as she chewed the inside of her lower lip. Her forehead was wrinkled across and down at the same time, like a dozen games of tic-tac-toe played over each other on the chalkboard and not erased very well. "Like what?" he asked.

Out of the corner of his eye, he saw Whiskers's head snap toward the kitchen. She got to her feet and growled low. "Whiskers," Toby said, reaching down to calm her. He looked toward the kitchen door and his hand froze in midair.

Mr. Bertram filled the doorway to overflowing, his stubby cigar twitching as it moved from one side of his mouth to the other. His hands hung down at his sides, making fists and relaxing as if he were squeezing out sponges. He teetered on the balls of his feet and glared at Toby and then at Whiskers.

"I thought so," he said through clenched teeth. "The retard and his bitch." A smile dented his doughy face. "Thought I was gone, eh?"

Toby's hands felt cold and light, as if they were suddenly drained of blood. Whiskers growled again, and Toby felt the touch of hair as it raised in hackles on her shoulders. He patted the hair, trying to smooth it down.

"Well, Momma, now we know who the cul-prit really

is." Mr. Bertram rocked from one foot to the other like a drunk boxer. "Nothing like catching the little retard red-handed."

Toby tried to stand, but his legs were rubbery and unresponsive.

"Don't try nothin'," Mr. Bertram growled, taking a step forward. "I locked the front door and latched all the windows. Stay put—both a ya—while I make a phone call."

Mr. Bertram followed his stomach as it swung around and teetered into the kitchen. Toby felt as if he'd been chased for a mile. His head was light and dizzy and his chest was tight. *What is this all about?* he asked himself in a tiny voice that bounced around inside his head. He strained to listen.

"Sheriff?" Mr. Bertram roared into the telephone. "Well, where is he? I'd like to report a break-in. This is George Bertram here. What? Where am I? I'm at 3618 Anne Street." Toby leaned forward in his chair and noticed that Mrs. Bertram was doing the same in her chair. "Look. You want my phone number you look it up in the book. I got a thief here in my house and I want the sheriff here. No. No, the twerp doesn't have a gun. Yes. I know who he is. He's the Thurston kid from next door. How should I know how old he is? The sheriff can find out when he gets here."

Toby felt Whiskers tense at the sound of Mr. Bertram's voice. "What?" The silence was long and tense. Toby's chin quivered. *He called me a thief. He thinks I've been taking things.* Toby looked at Mrs. Bertram.

Her face swam before him in tears that broke over the edge like a spent wave and trickled down his cheek. Toby brushed them away with the back of his hand.

"The sheriff won't be here for another hour? He's at an accident takin' pretty pictures?" Mr. Bertram was bellowing into the phone. "Your deputy is sick and the other one's on his dinner hour? Bet you'd sing a differnt tune if I was the mayor." Toby heard Mr. Bertram mutter something he couldn't make out. And then the bell inside the phone shuddered as Mr. Bertram slammed down the receiver.

Toby looked up as Mr. Bertram filled the doorway like a bear in a stretched-out human costume. Whiskers stood up, tense and alert. Mr. Bertram's cigar was gone—eaten during his angry conversation with the sheriff's office. Toby noticed a stained dent in Mr. Bertram's lower lip where the cigar usually rested.

"You're a lucky little bastard." Mr. Bertram's jaw muscle was flexing as he ground his back teeth. "I've half a mind ta take you over my knee and wallop the livin' daylights outta ya," he growled. "Guess I should call Olsen. He's always lookin' after you."

Toby watched Mr. Bertram turn back to the kitchen. He didn't know what was going on. Why was Mr. Bertram acting like this? He only came over to visit Mrs. Bertram.

"Olsen? Bertram here. Yes, been a long time since you heard my voice. Listen careful now. I got me a little problem that the sheriff's too busy for. An' I think you can help me."

Toby shut his eyes. He didn't want to hear what Mr. Bertram was going to say next, but he listened. "You seem to have special inter'st in the retarded family next door. . . . Listen. Don't get high and mighty with me, Olsen. I know a retard when I see one and I don't call 'em somethin' else. Look. I caught the Thurston kid in my house after he thought I went to work. Now we've had at least one break-in with things stole right out from under my momma's nose. . . . Yes. I drove off like always and walked back."

He tried to trick me, Toby thought.

"Olsen, you better come get him soon or the sheriff will be here. . . . Save that preachin' fer Sunday. Just git here." The bell inside the phone shuddered again as Mr. Bertram slammed down the receiver. Toby opened his eyes and looked up.

Mr. Bertram stalked back to the doorway. Toby felt like a cornered dog. Make one move toward me, he thought, and I'll skedaddle around you and out the door before you can swing your big belly around. Or I'll bite your ankle.

Mr. Bertram stood, not moving, staring at Toby and Whiskers. Toby tried to stare back at him, but his head shook and his eyes burned from not blinking. He dropped his head and closed his eyes. He felt as if he were shrinking into the darkness and that time was carrying him farther and farther away, making him smaller and smaller.

"What you did was the lowest of the low—takin' advantage of my momma, who can't even take care of herself. Whad'ya do with it?" Mr. Bertram sounded far away but Toby heard him take one step forward and stop.

"With what?" Toby's voice squeaked. He opened his eyes again and the sudden light made him feel as if he exploded to his normal size again.

"The radio!" Mr. Bertram bellowed. He folded his arms and rested them on the rounded top of his stomach. He rocked from foot to foot.

"I don't know . . . what you're talking about," Toby said, fear straightening his back. He realized his face was frozen into a grimacing smile. He quickly swallowed and pressed his mouth into a straight line.

" 'Course you do!" Mr. Bertram took another menacing step forward. "You took it right off Momma's dresser. You took it and you know it, you little . . ."

Rapping came from the front door, sounding like a giant woodpecker. Mr. Bertram kept his eyes on Toby. "Don't move," he growled, walking toward the door.

Mr. Bertram unlocked the door and flung it open with a grunt. Reverend Olsen's hand, raised to knock again, fell to his side. "Hello, Bertram," he said. "May I come in?"

Without a word Mr. Bertram turned around and walked to his mother. He stood behind her chair.

Reverend Olsen walked in and looked gravely at Toby. Toby slumped into his chair and stared back, noticing Reverend Olsen's clerical collar was stained with sweat where his throat met his jaw.

"I've tried to get this brat to tell me where he put

the radio he stole from my momma. Like talkin' to a brick wall. Like talkin' to his old man." He put his hands on his mother's shoulders. She shuddered and stared at Reverend Olsen.

"Ooooo," she moaned. "What is a man of the cloth doin' here? Come to wave crosses at me and put my wanderin' soul to rest? What is he here fer? Gonna mistake me fer a devil and say the Lord's Prayer backward to get rid of me? Ooooo." She tried to get up, but her son held her down.

"Quiet, Momma," he said. "He's here to take the boy away. Not you. Jes' that nasty boy and his bitch there."

Mrs. Bertram's big eyes turned to look at Toby. "He's a ghosty, like me. He ain't done nothin' wrong. Jes' a wanderin' spirit, looking fer some comfort . . . same's me."

"Jesus Christ," Mr. Bertram muttered. He glared at Reverend Olsen. "Momma's a little confused these days. Nothin' to worry about so we don't need your help or any more noses in our business. Jes' git the boy out. And that dog too. And if I ever catch them two in here agin, you'll have to pick 'em up with a shovel and cart 'em out. Hear?"

"Don't go!" Mrs. Bertram stared glassy-eyed at Toby and struggled to get up. "Don't go with that man! He'll put you six feet under, I swear he will. And I'll never see you agin!"

"Momma, Momma, Momma." Mr. Bertram held his mother down and tried to sound gentle. But the words stuck in his throat like fish bones and he coughed them up. "Momma! Let me git you a little somethin' to drink, Momma, to calm ya down."

"Don't!" Mrs. Bertram screeched. The veins on the side of her neck popped out big as garter snakes with the effort of trying to stand. Her legs wobbled and her arms strained to straighten.

Reverend Olsen looked down at Toby. "Let's go, Toby," he said quietly. Before he knew it, Toby was lifted out of the chair by his arm and propelled toward the door. Whiskers was right at his heels. Not letting go of Toby, Reverend Olsen reached around him and pulled the door closed.

"You've done it this time," Reverend Olsen said grimly, marching Toby down the sidewalk and cutting across the lawn toward Toby's house. Toby's arm was falling asleep below Reverend Olsen's grip.

"I didn't do anything," Toby muttered, tripping over one of Whiskers's half-chewed bones hidden in the grass and skipping on his other foot to keep his balance.

Reverend Olsen was silent. He marched up the stairs, his grip so sure that Toby glided upward, his feet barely touching the curled boards. Reverend Olsen stopped in front of the door and rapped. Toby stood dazed in front of his own front door, feeling like a stranger.

The door opened and his father's face appeared, looking soft and blurry through the mesh of the screen door.

Before Toby's father could say anything, Reverend Olsen stepped back and said, loudly and distinctly,

"Would you please come out here? I have something to say."

Toby squirmed to get away from Reverend Olsen, but the Reverend just tightened his grip and gave Toby's arm a little shake. Toby's fingers tingled from lack of blood.

Toby's father stepped out onto the porch, still in his work clothes. Toby smelled the sourness of the slaughterhouse and saw sweat stains running from his father's armpits down his shirt. "Hello, Reverend," he said, his face tired but smiling. "Howdy do?"

"Your neighbor, Mr. Bertram, just caught Toby inside his house. Apparently Toby has been inside before and taken some things. I want you to know that this is very serious." Reverend Olsen glared at Toby. "Very serious indeed. Mr. Bertram called the sheriff. And if they get involved I don't know if I'll be able to keep the social workers away. And you know what *that* means."

Foster homes, Toby thought, shuddering. They'll try to put me in a foster home.

Toby didn't want to see the hurt look on his father's face. He didn't want to see the sadness in his eyes or his struggle to say the right thing to Reverend Olsen. But, shy with shame, Toby looked up anyway and saw his father looking at him.

"Toby," his father slowly said, as if his name were a difficult word. "You take things from Mr. Bertram's house?"

Toby felt tears coming again. He swallowed the saltiness and shook his head. He sucked in his lower lip to keep it from quivering.

"You sure now?" His father's eyes didn't blink as he gazed into Toby's eyes. "Didn't borrow nothin' neither?"

"I didn't take anything, Papa," Toby said, his voice unsteady. "Or borrow."

"Toby," Reverend Olsen said sharply. "Don't you know what happens to boys who lie? And you know where the bad place is. You don't want to go there now, do you?" Reverend Olsen's voice was as tight as the grip on Toby's arm and Toby felt tightness growing inside him and a pressure building and building in his chest.

"I didn't do it!" Toby cried, twisting his arm and jerking away from Reverend Olsen. Reverend Olsen grabbed at Toby—too late. He was left with a fistful of air, looking as though he were going to punch Toby in the face. Slowly he lowered his arm.

Reverend Olsen's face froze into a mask that hid all of his emotions. In the dim light only his eyes looked real. "Toby, I pray you didn't, but I think you know better. I want you to think about what you've done. And I want you to return that radio to Mr. Bertram."

Reverend Olsen looked at Toby's father. "I know how hard you try. But Toby is going wild. He's done some things that are hard to explain. I think you should punish him for stealing from the Bertrams."

"He said he didn't do it," Toby's father said quietly. "He says he didn't do it, then he didn't."

"Mr. Thurston," Reverend Olsen began, "I don't want to threaten you, but you should know that Toby can be taken away from you."

Calmly and gently, Toby's father reached toward Toby and pulled Toby against him. Toby smelled hog blood as he pressed his ear against his father's side. The smell was strong and filled his head. "Toby is a good boy." His father's voice sounded deeper coming through his father's chest. "Ain't nobody gonna take him away."

Turning around, Toby and his father walked toward the screen door with Whiskers at their heels.

"I'll call the sheriff and tell him not to come this time," they heard Reverend Olsen say. "But if this happens again, I don't know but what he shouldn't get involved."

6

Reverend Olsen's threat hung heavy in the kitchen, hovering like the dense smell of their macaroni and cheese supper. Toby and his parents ate in silence. The stringy cheese stuck Toby's tongue to the roof of his mouth each time he chewed. Toby kept his eyes on his plate and listened to the food mushing around in his mother's mouth and his father's soft grunt each time he swallowed.

Whiskers lay next to Toby's chair, her eyes following each forkful of food from the plate to Toby's mouth. Her ears were cocked forward and her mouth was drawn up into a dog smile. Toby pinched a piece of macaroni and dropped it onto the floor between her front legs. Her tongue darted out and snatched it—like a frog nabbing a fly.

Mr. Thurston cleared his throat loudly and Toby looked up from Whiskers. His father stared at him, a mixture of sadness and curiosity shining in his eyes. *He should scold me for feeding Whiskers at the table,* Toby thought. *He always does. And it's right.* But his father didn't say anything and Toby dropped his gaze to the curls of macaroni snuggling against each other. He suddenly wished he were curled up under the porch and snuggling against Whiskers.

They can't take me away. He swallowed and the lump of food crept down his throat, catching in his chest somewhere near his heart. He gulped some milk and wiped the white mustache from his upper lip with the back of his left hand. As his hand returned to his lap, Whiskers lifted her head and sniffed, her tail wagging hopefully. *Later,* he told her with his eyes. *I'll feed you later.*

Toby waited until his parents finished eating and then quietly got up. He cleared the table, dodging around the unsteadiness of his mother and unsure shadow of his father, and began pouring hot water into the sink.

"Go on, Toby," his father said, his voice husky and tired. "Go on and play."

Toby looked at his mother. Her lips were turned in and pressed against her teeth. She nodded slowly, as if her neck hurt when she moved it. Toby knew what was causing the pain. It wasn't her neck. *Reverend Olsen is a poop,* he thought. And without a word, Toby put down the bottle of dish soap that always reminded him of a lady in a long dress with puffy sleeves and a tiny, tiny head. He scuffed across the kitchen, through the living room, and out the door.

The screen door shut quietly and the porch boards complained sleepily, like bedsprings, as Toby walked across the porch and down the steps. He stopped at the edge of the patch of light that looked as if it were painted onto the sidewalk and grass in the distorted shape of the door. To keep tears from spilling out, he closed his eyes and tipped his head back. He took a deep breath of the dark-flavored air and opened his eyes. The stars swam across the sky, as if reflected on the surface of a quiet lake. Toby blinked. Strewn across the sky, each star was now as sharp as the cricket chirps coming from under the porch. They were scattered every which way in a jumble—like his feelings.

His eyes swept across the sky and clumps of stars began to take shape: the Big Dipper balanced on its handle and, above it, the Little Dipper so faint Toby had to blink several times and strain his eyes to see it. As the stars drew themselves into familiar patterns, Toby's thoughts gathered together and became clearer.

I didn't do it. Toby stared at the Milky Way, his eyes lingering on a single star close to the edge. *But I'll find out who did.* Whiskers brushed the sidewalk with her tail.

Toby looked over to the Bertrams' house. The curtains were drawn and slivers of light sliced through the gaps where the curtains almost came together. Satisfied that Mr. Bertram was at work and that nobody was watching him, Toby turned toward the side of the porch and crawled under.

Whiskers nested between his stomach and his knees, and Toby listened to the faint voices of his parents as they talked in the kitchen.

"That's what Reverend Olsen said." His father's voice was pinched.

Toby strained to hear his mother's voice. "Rev'ran Ol-sin doesn' know every-thang."

"Maybe yer folks is right." His father's voice was thick and teary. "Maybe we should give 'im up. Or maybe send 'im to my folks. They's good to 'im."

"No." His mother's voice was clear and forceful. "To-bee is a-our son. We love 'im. We need 'im." Her voice grew stronger with each word. "An' he . . . needs . . . us."

A pan clattered onto the floor. Toby pictured them hugging each other—his father tall with arms like a grasshopper's and his mother looking like a rag doll torn and carelessly sewn back together. Toby pictured them hugging and wished he were with them—feeling the boniness of his father's hips and the pillow softness of his mother. He reached around Whiskers and, lifting her off the ground, he hugged hard, squeezing a breath from her. He tried not to cry.

Toby heard footsteps shuffling toward the bedroom.

And, branching from them, footsteps advanced toward the front door. The footsteps stopped before they were directly overhead.

"Toby?" his father called softly. "To-*bee.*" Toby held his breath. "Whar is that boy?" his father muttered, turning and walking back toward the bedroom.

Whiskers untangled herself from Toby's hug and sat up, panting softly.

"Sorry, Whiskers," Toby whispered, remembering that he still hadn't fed her.

As he poked his head out, Toby looked at the Bertrams' house. Nothing had changed. Light still glowed through all the curtains pulled across the windows and slices of light still escaped from gaps in the curtains. Toby pictured Mrs. Bertram inside drinking bug juice. Or hiding behind the couch.

I'll find out who took her radio, Toby thought, turning toward the porch steps. I'll find that radio and give it back to her.

At school Toby pretended he was the ghost Mrs. Bertram thought he was. He walked around invisible and silent and he felt as if nobody noticed him. But during the noon recess, as Toby was watching other kids play, the soccer ball careened toward him. Without thinking, Toby stopped it with his foot and picked it up. Harold ran up to him, red in the face and panting. A bead of sweat rolled down his forehead and caught in the corner of his eye. Harold blinked and rubbed at his eye with his knuckle.

Harold glared at Toby with his other eye. "Hand it over, retard," he wheezed. He took a lurching step toward Toby. He bent over, grabbed both knees with his hands, and shook his head back and forth. He looked up, his eyebrows arching, straining to see through the tatters of hair fluttering over his eyes. "Give me the ball, you little toad."

Toby's insides crawled. Robin trotted up. Her chest continued to bounce for a few moments after she stopped. Toby noticed an old-fashioned brooch pinned to her sweater below her shirt collar. It framed a faded photo that looked more like coffee stains than a face. But it was a face. A woman's face.

"What is this?" Robin asked, looking at Harold and Toby. "A little prayer meeting?" She grinned and Harold scowled. "Come on. Everybody's waiting."

Robin held out her hands for the ball. Toby looked up from the brooch. He blushed realizing she may have thought he was staring at her breasts.

"That's nice," he said, glancing at the brooch again. The frame looked like ivy.

"Thanks," she said, smiling. "Harold gave it to me."

Toby handed the ball back to her and she tossed her head, flipping her hair back. "Want to be on our team?" She combed her fingers through her hair.

"You kidding?" Harold stood up. "Leave this little freak out of it." He snatched the ball from her and ran back to the other kids, who were milling around on the field that stretched between the playground fences as lumpy and stained-looking as an old sleeping bag.

"Don't mind him," Robin said. Tongue-tied, Toby stared at her as she trotted back to the game.

Toby was afraid that Harold might be waiting for him after school because of what happened on the playground. But he decided to take a chance and go home with everybody else. He had work to do. Toby had decided to watch over the Bertrams' house and catch whoever had been taking things from Mrs. Bertram.

That afternoon, he and Whiskers began their watch from under the porch. He peered through the lilacs until Mr. Bertram roared off to work. And then he snuck around to the other side of the Bertrams' house. He sat in a thicket of Chinese elms by the alley. Each year the elms were chopped down and each year they grew back thicker than before. Hidden in the thicket Toby watched the far side of the Bertram house. To Toby, this side of the house was as new and mysterious as the dark side of the moon.

Mrs. Bertram's bedroom was on this side of their house and its window was open. As he sat in the thicket he heard Mrs. Bertram singing snatches of songs that sounded made up.

"My son he loves me. He loves me. He loves me."

Her voice was that of a little girl, off-key but pure as light through a newly washed window with a crack across it. And the tune followed her breathing, a note for each word—a high note when she began a new breath followed by lower and lower notes as her air ran out.

Toby shrank into the thicket and Whiskers lifted her

head as the back of Mrs. Bertram's head and shoulders appeared in the open window. She raised a brush to her wispy hair.

"My brush it loves me. It loves me. It loves me."

She turned her back to the window and Toby watched her, embarrassed, as she brushed the tattered shreds of white hair on the back of her head. He cringed, hoping that she wouldn't pull it out like the clumps of hair he brushed from Whiskers in the spring when she shed.

"What's a body to do?" She turned abruptly to the window. Her voice tensed and relaxed like a guitar string being tuned to breaking. "Even though I'm a-walkin' through that shadow in the valley that's dead"—she stuck her head out the window and peered squint-eyed at the garbage cans leaning against each other in the alley—"I fear no evil. My rod and my staff, they comfort me." She scanned the alley from left to right, and Toby felt her gaze pass over him like a powerful spotlight. She opened her mouth wide and gulped air. "An' that's 'cause I'll use that rod and staff to beat the tar out a any lily-livered brat comes near me agin!"

She withdrew her head from the window, bumping it, and pulled the window closed with a thump.

Toby sat quietly for a few minutes, stunned. I wonder if she means me? he thought. Or if she's thinking of somebody else?

The next evening Toby overheard Mr. Bertram talking into the telephone. Toby was just coming out onto the porch. He froze when he heard Mr. Bertram's voice as it rumbled through the open kitchen window. "Gotta go to work now," Toby heard. "Listen. Just keep it in mind. The old bat's crazy. She's lettin' some neighborhood brat steal her blind. Next thing you know *I'll* be missin' stuff. If I don't get rid of 'er, I'll go crazy. Rentin' her room to you will help me pay for the nursing home."

Toby slipped over the banister and dropped behind the lilac bushes. He motioned for Whiskers to stay.

"Listen," he heard Mr. Bertram growl. "Maybe you're too ornery. Just forget it. Yeah. You heard me." And the phone clattered into its cradle.

Toby crouched lower. Mr. Bertram is going to put his mother into a nursing home? And he's blaming me, saying that I steal from her and she lets me? That's like Reverend Olsen wanting to put me in a foster home, Toby thought.

Toby felt a new bond between himself and Mrs. Bertram. He realized how much he would miss her if she were ever taken away.

Maybe I should warn her, he thought. Naw, he decided. She wouldn't be able to do anything even if she knew. I know what Reverend Olsen wants to do and there's nothing I can do if he comes to take me away. Except kick and scream and bite.

Toby smiled picturing the fight Mrs. Bertram would put up if they came to take her away. She'd scream loud enough to wake up the dead, he thought.

Toby slipped under the porch. "Whiskers," he whispered upwards. He heard Whiskers's nails click on the wood as she walked across the porch and down the steps. Light from outside disappeared as she came under the porch.

The Bertrams' screen door slammed open and shut. Toby peered out through the lilacs and saw the car roar to life and charge down the driveway leaving behind a black cloud of exhaust.

Who's crazier, Toby wondered—Mrs. Bertram or Mr. Bertram? Harold's mean crazy and Reverend Olsen is sicky-sweet, goody-goody crazy, he thought. And Mom and Papa, they're crazy. And me? he wondered. Am I crazy?

Maybe crazy is normal, Toby thought, reaching over to Whiskers. Maybe everybody's crazy. He felt the softness of her ear points. You're not crazy. Yet. He patted her head to rattle her brain and sighed.

For a week and a half, nothing unusual happened at the Bertrams' house—except that Mr. Bertram's car broke down and he had to walk to work every evening. Twice, Mr. Bertram forgot that his car was broken. He would throw himself into the driver's seat and turn the key. When nothing happened but metallic wheezes and groans he would bang on the steering wheel, roll out onto his feet, and walk like a pregnant bear on its hind legs down the driveway and up the street.

On Wednesday Toby arrived just in time to see Mr. Bertram hanging laundry. Toby watched Mr. Bertram reach for the line, balancing on tiptoe like a hippopotamus doing ballet, taking gooey, stained clothespins out of one side of his mouth while maneuvering his cigar around on the other.

On Friday, Toby went to the library to say hi to Mrs. Windish. He only meant to say hi. But she corralled him and, before he could escape, he was shelving books next to her, listening to her describe each book she put on the shelf.

"Oh, Toby, you would enjoy this one. You really must start reading more." She turned to him and looked over her reading glasses. "This book is about three animals—a cat and two dogs, if I remember—and how they walked hundreds of miles back to their home, encountering many dangers along the way. Sometimes I'm just floored at the way animals attach themselves to people. If something happened to me, my dog would probably die before it would let anybody else feed it. . . ."

Toby shelved books for another twenty minutes, listening and not talking. But on the way home he thought about the first book she described. Would Whiskers let somebody else feed her if something happened to me? he wondered. If I died or went to a foster home, he thought, I wouldn't want her to die.

On the other hand, Toby couldn't help feeling jealous thinking about somebody else feeding Whiskers if he were dead or gone. He didn't want Whiskers to die of loneliness. But he didn't want Whiskers to look at somebody else the same way that she looked at him—with her brown eyes soft and trusting, her ears forward with one tip flopped over, her dog smile, and her delicate pink tongue hanging out just a little and moving slightly in and out and in and out as she breathed through her mouth.

How would he feel if something happened to Whiskers? The thought struck him like jumping into cold water. He and Whiskers were the same age. They were pups together, just like Grandfather Thurston said.

He was thinking these thoughts when he walked up the sidewalk to his house—a confused feeling of guilt and sadness about dying and about Whiskers and the two dogs and the cat that traveled hundreds of miles to get back home.

He saw Whiskers sitting at the bottom of the porch steps. Her tail was wagging and she sat tense, jerking forward and then stopping herself, waiting for Toby to signal for her to come. The confusion melted away inside him and he felt only the love they shared.

Toby stopped and patted his right thigh. Whiskers tore down the sidewalk and reared onto her hind legs. She planted her front paws on Toby's shoulders and licked him in the face.

He turned his face and wiped his mouth on his shirt sleeve. "Whiskers! Don't get mushy!"

But before he pushed her down onto her own four feet, Toby reached around her scruffy neck and gave her a hug.

"Come on," Toby said, reaching down playfully to grab her tail, now going faster than a windshield wiper on high. They walked down the sidewalk toward the house.

As they approached the porch steps, Toby heard a loud cackling noise coming from the Bertrams' house.

"What are ya doin'? Git away from there! Come on. Or I'll swat you agin with this broom!"

Mrs. Bertram was screaming and whooping and her voice came from first one open window and then another in the house. Toby heard bumps—some muffled and some not—and footsteps and a crash like glass breaking. Toby scurried around the porch and dove under it. Whiskers was a streak behind him. They lay panting, four wide eyes watching the Bertrams' house through the lilacs.

The screen door to the kitchen popped open and Toby saw Pete back out onto the steps.

"Aw come on, Harold," he whined. "Let's go."

"Gotcha!" he heard Mrs. Bertram cry and then laugh. "Gotcha agin!"

Harold exploded onto the porch and bumped into Pete. He was red-faced and clutching something in his arms, like a football. "Watch it, you old biddy!" he yelled, his voice cracking. Pete stumbled down the steps and John flew out the door, bumping into Harold. He was cradling a jar in his arm.

"Let's get outta here!" he said, breathlessly. And together John and Harold and Pete ran down the steps, barely in control.

Mrs. Bertram charged out the door, a broom resting on her shoulder like a baseball bat. She raised it in the air like a flag and yelled, "Jes' wait 'til you're dead." Toby gasped as she took a tottering step forward and almost stepped off the stoop. "I'll git ya then. Jes' wait. I'll git ya then."

Abruptly she turned back toward the house, smacking the doorjamb above her with the broom as she marched in.

Toby crawled out from under the porch into the sudden silence. He ran, hunched, to the back of his house, and peered around the corner. He saw John disappear down the alley. A little cloud of dust puffed up with each pounding step.

Still hunched, Toby ran to the alley. He looked around the rancid-smelling garbage cans that had been building heat inside all day and saw John dart into a backyard to the left.

Toby and Whiskers sprinted down the alley to the cover of the next group of garbage cans.

"Wait up!" he heard John yell. And Toby followed the direction of his voice into a backyard.

Toby ran behind a car parked on the street and was ready to bolt across when he looked up toward the Lutheran church. He saw Harold, Pete, and John jogging up the lawn in front of the church and around the corner.

Toby raced up the street and across the church lawn. He caught himself with both hands on the corner of the church, around which the boys had disappeared, banging his chest against the white boards with chipped paint. Peeking around the corner, he saw half a cellar door gently fall until it was even with the other half.

7

Toby and Whiskers took the long way home, by way of the railroad tracks. When they got to the tracks, Toby heard the faint rumble of an approaching train. They stood beside the tracks and listened. Soon the rails hummed with energy. The train rounded the bend and a blast of air and noise hit them like a slap across the face as the train barreled by. And then, as fast as it came, the train was gone—around the bend and out of sight. The rails were left tingling, like the hair on the back of Toby's head.

Toby sighed and stepped onto a rail. With Whiskers stepping on the ties beside him, Toby walked down the track. He watched his shoes cover the rail, one after another, and thought about what he had seen at the church. His thoughts, like the train, were unswerving, thundering through his head at fearful speed. *I know where the radio is. I know who took it. They took even more than that. I have to figure out a way to get it all back.*

Toby looked up from his feet and his thoughts derailed. He realized that, for the first time in his life, he was walking effortlessly on a rail. His arms flew out level with his shoulders and dipped left and then right, like an airplane banking back and forth, out of control. He fought to keep his balance, but the harder he fought the more he lost control.

"Whoa!" he gasped, and Whiskers skittered away, tail between her legs, before Toby stumbled and landed on the cinders where she had been.

Toby picked himself up and examined the cinder dents in the skin of his palms. Whiskers sniffed at Toby's knees and licked where he was scraped under his jeans.

Toby patted Whiskers on the head. "Thanks, girl," he said and hopped over several ties. He veered to the left, into some bushes cut flat for the trains. Toby felt like a ghost disappearing through a wall and thought of Mrs. Bertram. He and Whiskers fought their way through grabby branches and cut across a vacant lot, doubling back toward the slaughterhouse where his father worked.

Whiskers raised her nose to the breeze and sniffed. Toby listened. The hulking cement building was as quiet as death. Toby spun around and ran, hoping to catch up to his father before he got home.

Too late, Toby thought, as he rounded the corner to his street. With Whiskers at his feet, Toby ran up the sidewalk and bounded up the stairs. He flung the door open, skidded to a stop, and almost fell over onto his face.

His mother and father were hugging and laughing and moving awkwardly around the floor as if they were dancing. His father hadn't changed his clothes yet. His mother's stomach stuck out enough so that, even though his father bumped up against her, he was far enough away to keep from stepping on her shuffling feet.

They turned and Toby's father saw him over the top of his mother's head.

"Toby!" he shouted. A dark patch of dried hog blood near his mouth cracked as his face broke into a wider grin. "Guess wha'?"

Toby's mother turned to look at him, her eyes gleaming, her chest heaving from the dancing. Little beads of sweat stood out on her forehead. As Toby looked, one bead in the middle of her forehead slipped and slid down the curve of her nose and hesitated for a moment before it fell off onto the shelf of her bosom.

"No, what?" Toby felt excitement building in his chest.

"Yer momma got herself a job!" his father announced.

"A job?" Toby asked.

"Wi' Rev'ran Ol-sin's halp," his mother said, nodding.

"He picked 'er up and took 'er to a intra-view," his father said, bobbing up and down in his excitement.

Toby ran up to his mother and gave her a hug.

"An' the bes' part is," his father said, pounding Toby on the back in his excitement, "she'll be workin' in yer school!"

Toby's arms lost their strength and he stepped back from his mother, puzzled. *At his school?*

"She'll be a-servin' you hot lunches!" his father continued. "An' bringin' home whatever's left fer ar' supper." He turned toward Toby's mother and put an arm around her shoulders. "Be like goin' out ta eat ever' night."

Toby ached to be proud and happy for his mother. He listened to his parents talk excitedly as he helped get supper ready. He told himself how nice his mother's job would be for all of them. More money. More food.

But after supper Toby retreated to the cool darkness under the porch and his true feelings closed in on him. Deep down, Toby was afraid of how the kids at school would react to his mother as she served up hot lunches.

Maybe she'll just be in back, putting food on the trays, he thought. Or washing the spoons. Or picking the spoons out of the garbage. Or washing trays.

But he pictured her standing behind the window from where lunches were served to each kid. He pictured her trying to talk to the kids. And kids laughing in her face.

Reverend Olsen is a poop, Toby thought. Always got his nose in the wrong place—like boy dogs with Whiskers. Why doesn't he just keep his nose out of our business?

All Monday morning, during math and reading and spelling, Toby was as nervous as a cat in a cage. He couldn't concentrate on anything—except lunch. When lunch came, he trudged down the hall, trailing his class, torn between hoping for the best and fearing the worst.

Harold was in the middle of the line talking with Robin. Toby watched Harold, keeping his head tilted down and glancing at him sideways. Toby glanced farther up the line and saw that everybody was picking up their trays of food just as always. He began to relax.

Harold was turned toward Robin when he stepped up to the window. Without taking his eyes off Robin, he reached for a tray, grabbing the corners nearest him. He lifted it and the tray flipped over with a dull clunk. Beans scattered over the edge of the counter and a few fell to the floor.

"Harold!" Robin exclaimed.

Harold turned toward the window. "Oh, excuse me!" he said with exaggerated horror. He peered at the person inside. "I'm so sorry. May I help you pick that up, Mrs. Thurston?"

Toby cringed at his mother's voice. "No, Har-old. I will ge' it."

Harold reached for a new tray. "Thank you, Mrs.

Thurston." And Harold leered at Toby before he walked away with Robin. The piece of garlic bread on his tray bounced up and down. Robin's eyebrows puckered and she frowned as she followed Harold with her tray. Several other kids looked back at Toby, puzzled expressions on their faces. Toby looked at his feet and shuffled toward the window with the line.

When he got to the window, Toby shyly looked in. "To-bee," his mother said, smiling.

"Hi," Toby mumbled as he picked up his tray and quickly walked away.

Toby rushed through lunch, barely chewing his food before he swallowed, and walked down the hall toward the double doors leading to the playground. His hands were jammed into his pockets. Through his pockets he fiddled with the bottom elastic band on his underwear and looked at the tops of his shoes. He put one foot directly in front of the other, as if he were walking on the train track, following a thin black line that separated the linoleum tiles.

He pushed the door's bar with his elbow and continued to walk with his head down as if the line between the tiles continued outside. Startled, he saw another pair of shoes in front of him, pointing toward him. Toby stopped before he stepped on them and looked up.

Harold was smirking, his hands on his hips. Toby turned his head slowly to the right and saw John grinning at him. Next to John was Pete, looking uncomfortable—as if his lunch had upset his stomach.

"Dad told us that he helped your old lady get a job at school," Harold said, shifting his weight from one foot to the other. "Good old Dad. Always trying to help out the re-turded family."

Toby ducked to his left and turned. But Harold stepped in front of him, blocking his way.

"You must be real proud of your old lady," Harold said with mock kindness. "She did a *wonderful* job," he continued, "dishing up those beans . . . putting the toast on top just so." Harold demonstrated, his little fingers arched, his other fingers dainty. "Everything looked *so* good. Didn't it?"

"Yeah, sure," said John. "Looked real good. Where'd she learn to cook, Toby?" John's voice was sly. "Meatball Community College?"

"And she cleaned up everything *so* nice," Harold continued. "That was so *nice* of her." Harold's face relaxed and his jaw dropped and his shoulders slumped and his eyes glazed with confusion. " 'No, Har-old. I will ge' it.' " Toby's ears tingled. Harold sounded just like his mother. His temples began to throb, and he squinted his eyes to slits.

Keeping his same posture, Harold smiled the lopsided smile of Toby's mother, turned awkwardly, and shuffled away. Toby held his breath. He felt his heart banging against his ribs as if it were trying to get out and pound on Harold.

"Come on," Pete said, looking more uncomfortable than before. "Let's play some soccer before recess is over." He glanced at Toby, his eyes wary and ashamed.

"Ho-kay," Harold said, thickly. "Ca' I be the sock-her bawl? Huh? Ca' I?"

Toby clenched his fists and leaped onto Harold's back, pressing his knees against Harold's side and flailing at the back of his head. Harold's legs crumpled and his knees thumped against the asphalt.

"Ow!" Harold grunted, trying to roll over onto his back, on top of Toby. Toby loosened his knees and let Harold roll over underneath him until he was sitting on Harold's stomach. Toby gritted his teeth and aimed for his nose, striking out again and again. Harold closed his eyes, turned his face, and held up his arms, crossed, to fend off Toby's blows.

"You crazy? Get off him." John grabbed Toby's shirt collar and yanked. Toby held tight with his knees. Slowly as a leech peels off skin Toby lost his hold on Harold. John pulled Toby to his feet. Toby twisted around to strike at John when Harold kicked Toby in the stomach. Toby doubled over and Harold kicked out again, barely missing Toby's face.

A whistle blew on the other side of the playground and Harold, John, and Toby froze. Slowly all three heads turned toward the sound of the whistle. They saw Mrs. Schell, the second grade teacher, hobble toward them, her tight skirt holding her knees close together and shortening her stride. John let go of Toby, who collapsed onto the asphalt next to Harold. Dazed, Toby was pleased to see Harold's knees, skinned and bleeding, poking out from tears where his jeans had popped open.

"What is going on here?" Mrs. Schell gasped, wobbling slightly on the heels of her pumps. "What do you youngsters think you're doing?" She tried to sound tough, but Toby could see in her darting eyes that she was not used to dealing with fifth grade boys and was afraid of them.

"He jumped on me," Harold said, scrambling to his hands and knees. He looked up at Mrs. Schell with his innocent eyes. "And then he started hitting me."

"Yeah, for no reason at all," said John. "I was trying to stop him."

Toby looked at Pete, who didn't say anything. Instead, Pete was kicking the asphalt with the heel of his right shoe.

Mrs. Schell looked at each boy, trying to size each one up. Her mouth hardened and her lips disappeared. "I think that you boys should have a talk with Mrs. Gunderson. You too," she said, looking at Pete.

"Aw shoot," Pete mumbled, looking down.

Toby stood up and Mrs. Schell grabbed his arm. She grabbed Harold with her other hand and marched into the building and down the hall toward the school office. John and Pete followed reluctantly.

Miss Buzbee, the school secretary, looked up as Mrs. Schell puffed into the office.

"May I help you, Mrs. Schell?" she asked, turning from her typewriter and facing them.

"These boys were fighting on the playground," Mrs. Schell replied. "I thought Mrs. Gunderson would like to speak with them."

"Mrs. Gunderson is meeting with a parent right now," Miss Buzbee said. "But have them sit over there"—she pointed toward a row of chairs backed up against the wall—"and I'll watch them until she's free."

"Thank you," Mrs. Schell said. She let go of Toby and Harold and clacked out of the office.

Harold slouched toward the corner chair. Pete and John followed him. Harold fell back into the chair and scootched his rear to the chair's edge. He crossed his arms and stared grumpily at Miss Buzbee.

Toby stared at the empty chair next to John and didn't move.

"Toby," said Miss Buzbee. "You may sit down if you want."

Toby just stood, his shoulders drooping, suddenly very tired. He felt in his gut what was going to happen. Like a kick to the stomach, Toby felt that Harold would come out smelling like a rose. As for himself, Toby felt that once again he would come out looking like a troublemaker with a screw loose. Maybe now they will take me away from my parents, he thought. If they do I'll come back like the animals in the book Mrs. Windish described. I'll find my mother and father even if they take me to Des Moines.

John threw his arm over the back of the empty chair and leaned toward it. "Come on. Sit down." He stared at Toby. "I won't bite 'cha." His smile showed straight white teeth, top and bottom.

Toby looked up at Miss Buzbee, not moving.

"Toby," she said, smiling. "I think Mrs. Gunderson

would be pleased if you waited in the library."

"Hey . . ." Harold sat bolt upright. He closed his mouth and glared at Miss Buzbee. She turned to Harold and looked at him coolly.

She stood up and walked around her desk to Toby. "Go on," she said, putting her hand against the small of his back and pushing gently. Toby locked his knees and leaned into Miss Buzbee's hand. "I'll come get you when Mrs. Gunderson wants to see you. Just tell Mrs. Windish I sent you."

Toby was afraid that Harold would try to get him for Miss Buzbee's special treatment. He could still sit next to John and show them he didn't want to be treated differently. But Toby wanted to be alone. More than anything, he wanted to be under the front porch with Whiskers. And if he couldn't be there, the library would do. Toby unlocked his knees and let Miss Buzbee guide him to the door.

Toby sat at a table tucked away in the library's corner, hidden from Mrs. Windish's gaze by a half-stack of shelves. Toby laid his head on his arms and closed his eyes. He felt like crying, and his nose started stuffing up. Through his mind flashed a time when he was in first grade and he had a cold and stuffed-up nose. He remembered sitting at this table—where he was right now—because it was out of the way and nobody could see him. He'd grabbed a book for older kids. Some of its pages had been glued together with brown, crusty stuff that looked like blood.

Toby snuffed in a drip coming down his nose and lifted his head. He scanned the shelves in front of him, trying to picture the book and remember the way it felt. The book was skinny, but not too skinny, he remembered, wiping his nose with the back of his hand. And the title had something to do with dead.

Toby's eyes stopped on a book called *Dorp Dead*. Toby quietly got up, walked around the table, and lifted the book off the shelf. He walked back to his chair and sat down.

Toby opened the book to the first page. Smeared across the page was the shiny, brownish stain. What is that? he wondered. Blood? Food?

He flipped through the book and saw several more pages that had been glued together. Toby turned to the back cover and looked at the pocket with the book's check-out card. He pulled the card from the pocket and looked at the signatures. He didn't recognize any of the names. The book hadn't been checked out for several years.

"That's a good book, Toby."

Toby jumped and dropped the book onto the table. He looked over his shoulder into Mrs. Gunderson's smiling face. He turned his head around and followed her out of the corner of his eyes as she walked around the table, pulled out a chair, and sat down. "You should read that book if you haven't already," she said, brushing back a wisp of white hair and hooking it behind her ear. "I think you'd like it."

Toby looked up at her through his eyelashes.

"You might even want to read it to your parents," she said. Mrs. Gunderson swallowed and the turkey skin of her neck rippled. "But right now, we have some things to discuss—just you and me." Her voice was kind but full of business. "And I'd like for you to look me straight in the eye." She reached over the table and, holding his chin, gently tilted Toby's head up. Toby stared at her, wide-eyed. He looked into her young, alert eyes, so different from her old, saggy face.

"That's better," she said, sitting back in her own chair. She crossed her legs and her nylon stockings rubbed together like sandpaper.

8

"I listened to Harold's side of the story—and John's and Pete's," Mrs. Gunderson began, her voice measured, giving each syllable equal time, "and now I'd like for you to tell me your side of the story. What happened out there on the playground, Toby?"

Toby looked down at the book on the table. His tongue felt as though it had fallen asleep. She's listened to Harold, he thought. She won't believe me now.

"Toby, I'd like for you to look at me," Mrs. Gunderson said firmly. Toby struggled to look at her. "I'd like you to tell me what happened on the playground after lunch. People don't fight without a reason."

Toby struggled not to look back at the book. His head shook with the effort of keeping it level. He pressed his lips together and his mouth flattened into a tight, silly grin that had nothing to do with his feelings. He tried not to blink and when he did his head and neck shuddered and his head dropped forward.

"You know, when I talked with Harold and then with John and then with Pete, their stories weren't at all the same," Mrs. Gunderson said. "In fact, they were quite different. And I don't think any of them told me the real reason why you jumped on Harold and started hitting him."

Toby closed his eyes. He saw his mother's face peering from the window and smiling her crooked smile. He felt ashamed that he hadn't been nicer to her. He imagined her face drooping like a tomato plant baking in the summer sun and hurt withering the happiness in her eyes. He'd almost been as cruel to his mother as Harold had been. He looked up from the book, straight into Mrs. Gunderson's face. The skin on her face, with its delicate wrinkles, looked as soft and strong as a well-worn, rumpled sheet.

Toby's chest heaved as he sucked air. His shoulders shook as he spoke. "They . . . made fun of . . . of my mom."

Mrs. Gunderson nodded, her earrings jiggling on her stretched-out earlobes. The wisp of white hair untucked from behind her ear and she brushed it back. "I thought so," she said. "When Miss Buzbee brought the four of you to the office I was chatting with your mother, asking her how her first day went."

Toby tried to swallow the fistlike tightness in his throat. The tightness grabbed harder.

"She was happy with her first day. She was expecting more trouble from kids than she got." Mrs. Gunderson studied Toby. "Toby, your mother did very well. But I can't say that surprised me. I've known your mother most of her life. She was a lovely, beautiful girl. In many, many ways she is still beautiful and lovely. It's just that her beauty is not where you can easily see it."

Mrs. Gunderson uncrossed her legs, nylon hissing against nylon, and leaned forward. She put her arms on the table and spoke more softly. "Reverend Olsen was right to think of your mother when I told him I needed another person to help with the school lunches. I should have thought of her myself."

Toby tensed. "Reverend Olsen should mind his own business," he mumbled, looking down.

"Pardon me?" Mrs. Gunderson asked, measuring each syllable.

Toby looked up. "Reverend Olsen should mind his own business. He should just leave us alone." Toby's voice shook. He waited for Mrs. Gunderson to get angry. Her eyes were steady and calm. "He wants to put me in a . . . a foster home," Toby said, more loudly. "And he believes everything Harold tells him. And Harold lies!"

Mrs. Gunderson nodded.

"Harold picks on me. And Reverend Olsen picks on Mom . . . and Papa. He makes them feel bad. He's always buttin' in, tellin' 'em what to do." His jaw clamped shut. Through his teeth Toby said, "I hate him!"

Toby felt a cramp knotting the bottoms of his feet and he relaxed his fisted toes. He panted, as if he'd just run from Harold.

Mrs. Gunderson sat back and placed her hands in her lap. She nodded. "Toby, I think there are some things you should know about Reverend Olsen . . . why Reverend Olsen looks after you and your dad and your mom." Mrs. Gunderson closed her eyes a moment, collecting her thoughts.

"I was your mother's English teacher at the high school here. Seems like a lifetime ago." She smiled and her eyes looked far away. "Your mother was a good student—not the best, but good. She was also very shy. Ralph—Reverend Olsen was just Ralph then—was in her class and during their junior year your mother and he became . . . sweethearts, I guess you'd say. At that time he was a swaggering, cocky young man—full of beans and life. He played all the sports because the high school was so small that every boy had to, otherwise there wouldn't be enough for full teams and nobody would get to play. And he was the star of them all."

Toby tried to imagine Reverend Olsen as a boy—and pictured Harold in a clerical collar.

"I think that Ralph was good for your mother. And she was good for him. Her grades didn't improve a whole lot but she became more outgoing. He seemed

to quiet down a little bit and wasn't quite as wild.
Toward the end of that year rumors started flying around
this little town that they were planning to be engaged
during their senior year and married when they graduated. I believed it. I never saw them apart. They did
everything together—and they were always laughing and
talking.

"That summer—between their junior and senior
years—your mother suffered the accident." Toby cringed.
He didn't want to hear about the accident again. Every
time his mother's parents visited they found a way to
fit "the accident" into the conversation. "She was helping her father in the fields, plowing the face of a hill
with the tractor. Somehow she slipped into a hole or
something sheared off in the rear wheel and the tractor
flipped over. It was just one of those crazy things. Your
mother was caught underneath. Nobody expected her
to live."

Toby felt his toes balling up again. His toenails dug
into the bottom of his shoes.

"Ralph took it very hard. He was a very angry young
man—angry with everybody and everything. He refused to visit your mother in the hospital while she was
in a coma. And even when she regained consciousness
he still didn't visit her. He must have been terribly afraid
of what he'd see or how he'd react. He dropped out of
football and for the first time in twenty years we didn't
have a football team. He refused to go out for basket-
ball and nobody got to play.

"But he was young. And during the spring, he went

out for track and he started dating again. He went off to college and decided to become a minister. He got married and graduated with honors. He could have gone anywhere to preach. But he came back here. For a long time, nobody here understood why.

"Toby, it's hard to understand other people—how they tick and what they're thinking. And sometimes you just never know. But it's my guess that Reverend Olsen still feels badly about your mother—and about never seeing her after the accident. It's my guess that he came back partly to make up for the hurt he may have caused your mother—that he helps your family because he feels guilty about that time."

Mrs. Gunderson studied Toby, cocking her head to one side. She saw a spent boy caught by this new knowledge, as afraid and exhausted as if this knowledge were quicksand. She saw pain in his tense little body—pain that comes from emotions drawn up tight as a charley horse. She'd been too wrapped up in the story to notice his suffering. And now she regretted telling him about Reverend Olsen and his mother.

"Toby," she said, suddenly feeling sad and tired, "Reverend Olsen means well. And if Harold makes fun of your mother again, just let me know. Now, you should go back to class before you miss the entire afternoon."

Toby sat stunned. His feet hurt and his head hurt.

"Go on, Toby, " Mrs. Gunderson said, standing up. She walked around the table and gently took Toby's arm. She helped him to his feet. He winced. "We're all proud of your mother, and I know she's proud of you."

Walking back to class, Toby felt sick—feverish and weak. He turned toward the first and second grade classrooms and walked out the door at the end of the hall. Almost as if he were wading in deep water, Toby struggled home, drowning in the things that Mrs. Gunderson told him. He tripped on curbs and blindly walked out into streets. He knew that Mrs. Gunderson had tried to help—to make him feel better about Reverend Olsen.

But Toby felt worse than ever. He wondered if his father knew that his mother and Reverend Olsen had been sweethearts in high school. That they had talked about getting married and that everybody thought that they would. He hated Reverend Olsen for being his mother's sweetheart. And then he hated Reverend Olsen for dropping his mother after the accident.

What if Reverend Olsen hadn't dropped my mother like that? Toby turned up his street. *Would I have been born? And if I had been born, would Reverend Olsen be my father? And would Harold be my brother?* A shiver shot up Toby's spine. Toby felt oddly related to Harold—as if they were brothers, as if now he could never escape Harold and Harold's meanness—any more than his mother and father could ever escape Reverend Olsen's nosy help.

His head hanging low, Toby walked up the sidewalk

to his house. He didn't see Whiskers sit up, surprised
that Toby was home early. Her tail was still, waiting
for his greeting, ready to spring. Exhausted, Toby walked
around the porch, dropped to his knees, and crawled
under. Whiskers watched him disappear and her ears
drooped. She closed her mouth and her dog smile disappeared. She walked down the porch steps and around
to the side. She stuck her nose into the darkness and
wagged her tail shyly, hoping that Toby was playing a
game.

Toby was curled up in a ball, his back toward her.
Whiskers walked up to him and sniffed the back of his
neck. Quietly she sat down on her haunches and lowered her front legs to the ground. Patiently she waited,
watching Toby's body heave and shudder as he cried.

That night, when Toby was sleeping on the bed that
pulled out from the couch, the old T-shirt he slept in
crept up and wound around his armpits and his underpants slipped down, tangling his ankles. Toby slept with
a frown, haunted by a dream that used to visit him
often. The dream hadn't visited Toby for a long time,
which made it as vivid and painful as sudden bright
light after a long darkness.

Toby saw himself clearly, as in a movie. And, at the
same time, he saw what was happening through his
dream-person's eyes. He saw himself, standing in slush,
in his T-shirt and underwear, wet snow falling like cloud
chunks on his bare head and pocking the slush around
him as it landed. He saw from his dream-person's eyes

the cars rushing by, throwing dirty snow and freezing water onto his legs.

Through his dream-person's eyes he looked down and saw that he was standing in the street, just off the curb, in his bare feet. The slush had pulled off his slippers as he stepped and he stared down in confusion not knowing what to do. Cars rushed by and gritty slush arched upward, pelting him.

Fear locked Toby's bones and wouldn't let him move. Toby didn't want to bend over to free his slippers from the slush because he was afraid cars would bang into his head. He didn't want to step back out of the way because he was afraid he would slip and fall.

Toby felt the cold bite at his toes and then his feet grew numb. His hands grew numb. And his head grew numb. He stared, helpless, as his feet turned red and then blue. People walked past him, coming and going, crossing the street. They didn't say a word. They stepped carefully around him, sneaking glances at his face, ashamed of what they saw.

Anguished, Toby cried out for help. A deep, animal grunt squeezed out from his mouth. He panicked and tried to raise one foot. The slushy water sucked, pulling it down. He couldn't move. He felt warmth spilling down his legs. He looked down and saw a yellow stain grow larger on the pouch of his underwear, and the little stream became a river that ran down his legs, warm and soothing, and then disappeared into the dirty slush around his ankles.

Toby closed his eyes and cried out again, and the

sound was muffled as if his mouth were stuffed with cloth. He lost his balance and began to fall—toward the cars rushing by, toward the tire-rutted slush, and he couldn't move his arms to catch himself.

With a start Toby woke, shaking, biting into the corner of his pillow. He lay still, his heart racing like the clickity-clack of a train rushing by in the distance. He blinked at the sudden darkness of the room.

He felt a warm, spreading wetness grow colder in the middle of the bed. He pulled the pillow from his mouth. The smell of warm urine filled the air, so strong he could almost taste it.

Toby hadn't peed in his sleep for a long time. And he felt ashamed.

9

After school Toby found a spot in some bushes with a good view of the church cellar. He and Whiskers burrowed through the branches so that he could watch without being seen. Trying to sit still in spite of the mosquitoes that swarmed around his ears, he shook his head, hoping that his tumble-down hair would keep them from landing on his neck and face. He slapped at a sharp jab on his chin, examined his palm, and saw nothing. The longer he watched, the more jabs he felt all over his body. When he moved, prickly bush branches poked through his clothes, feeling like mosquitoes. He shook his hair and swatted between his shoulder blades and at the small of his back, trying to keep his elbows from hitting branches and shaking leaves. But for each mosquito he killed many more seemed to find him in the cool green of the bushes. He scratched a spot on his forearm and a rounded, red welt popped up. He scratched the welt until it bled.

Out of the corner of his eye, Toby saw half of the cellar door lift. John's head poked up and his eyes scouted back and forth. John opened the door wider and held it open for Harold and Pete. The three of them eased the door down. They slunk around the far side of the church and across the backyard.

Toby slowly counted to ten and crept out of the back side of the bushes. He peered around at grass level to make certain Harold, John, and Pete weren't lurking nearby. He stood up, stiff from sitting in the bushes so long, and looked around some more. He and Whiskers scurried to the cellar doors and Toby grabbed one by its corner. He grunted as he strained to lift it and slowly, with a groan, it creaked open. Dropping onto his knees, Toby hoisted the door to his shoulder and struggled to his feet.

"Come on," he quietly told Whiskers. The dog sat to one side, avoiding his face and his voice. She lay down and put her head on her paws. "All right for you," Toby said. He stepped onto the top cellar stair and, sliding the door along his shoulder, closed it over his head by walking down.

The darkness swallowed him up as the door shut out the afternoon light. The dusty smell of the cellar reminded Toby of the smell underneath the porch, but something about the air wasn't soothing. Toby wrinkled his nose and sniffed like Whiskers would. He caught a whiff of cigarette smoke.

A dim light filtered through a tiny cellar window. Toby's eyes grew used to the foggy darkness and shapes slowly formed, emerging like ghosts from the shadows. The floor of the cellar was dirt. And from the dirt poked several rows of stout wooden beams that propped up the floor above. To his left, Toby saw long tables with legs folded underneath them like dead bug legs, leaning with their backs against the wall. Folding chairs of gray steel leaned in long rows against the wall in front of him. Stenciled in block letters on the underside of the flipped-up seats was PROPERTY OF THE PRAIRIE-VIEW LUTHERAN CHURCH. Underneath that was stenciled, in smaller letters: THOU SHALT NOT STEAL.

To his left Toby saw cardboard boxes, stacked haphazardly like a mountain range, two peaks touching the floor above. As Toby walked toward the boxes the cigarette smoke grew thicker. He slipped through a small gap between the boxes and a wall and found himself in a small space, hemmed in by walls and boxes and a large, black furnace. Another small cellar window let in dull light through which specks of dust wandered in and out.

On the walls hung posters of bigger-than-life faces of leering rock stars with glassy eyes. The corners of the posters curled outward and their middles poofed from the wall like little bellies, bloating and distorting the faces. An old mouse-eaten mattress sprawled in the corner, its soiled stuffing growing from holes like mold. A candle was stuck into its own drippings near the mattress and the warm shiny wax near the wick was just forming a dull skin.

Toby felt uncomfortable, as if the eyes on the walls were following him when he moved. Mice scurrying in the dark edges of the room sounded like the poster people whispering. Toby turned slowly around, his hands ready to strike, and saw an old radio sitting on an un-opened box. Its dial was a smiling mouthful of broken teeth framed by knobs that looked like dimples. Toby stepped closer and saw a jar full of coins at the base of the box.

He ran his fingers over the top of the radio. Its smooth wooden veneer shone with boldly striped grain. Toby stopped to examine the jar of coins. The coins were pennies, some tarnished to blackness. Others, he was surprised to see, were silvery.

The jar was heavy, but Toby cradled it in the crook of one arm. He leaned over and carefully gathered the radio into the crook of his other arm. He walked around the wall of boxes and up the steps until his head bumped the doors. Dipping his head, he took another step up until the door rested on the round of his back and shoulder. He grimaced and took another step and pushed with his legs, feeling pressure build on his shoulder. The door slowly rose and fresh air streamed around his face. Toby slid his shoulder, scraping along the door as he walked up the steps and into the light.

Toby carefully set the radio on the other cellar door and maneuvered around so that he could set the jar next to the radio. The door ground into the back of his neck. He stepped up onto the grass and struggled to ease the door down. With a foot more to go, the door slipped from his fingers and fell, echoing hollowly through the cellar and church. Toby scooped up the jar and radio and ran for cover, his heels kicking the radio's plug that flapped behind him.

Mr. Bertram's car was in the driveway pointed toward the street, its grille and bumper sneering at Toby as he and Whiskers walked up the driveway. Toby walked by the car as cautiously as he would walk around a strange dog.

Toby walked toward the Bertrams' kitchen door and Whiskers followed, her tail falling limp between her legs.

Toby and Whiskers stood at the bottom of the kitchen steps. Toby took a deep breath, not knowing what to do next. He swallowed nervously and looked up at the battered screen door, dented near the bottom where Mr. Bertram kicked it open.

As he looked, the kitchen door opened and filled with Mr. Bertram's bulk. Mr. Bertram was looking back inside the house. " 'Bye now, Momma. Be back after work."

He turned and pushed open the screen door with his belly and started lumbering down the stairs. He saw Toby and Whiskers and teetered to a stop.

"What the hell . . . ?" His cigar froze in his dented lips and his eyes bulged. Anger replaced the surprise on his face and he squinted down at them. "What the hell are you doing with that radio?" he shouted, pointing at Toby with a finger that looked like a half-chewed cigar. Whiskers stepped toward Toby, her body tense. "And that," his finger shifting to the jar. "What's that!"

Toby's knees felt weak and he opened his mouth to speak.

"So I was right after all," Mr. Bertram bellowed. "You *did* take that radio. And somethin' else too. Why, you mangy li'l runt!" Whiskers leaned into Toby's leg and growled deeply.

Keeping an eye on them, Mr. Bertram turned his head toward the kitchen and scrunched his mouth to the side. "Momma!" he called. "Momma, come 'ere!"

He faced Toby and Whiskers, his face flushing red as an overripe tomato.

Toby gulped a mouthful of air. He looked up at Mr. Bertram through his eyelashes. "I found these and brought 'em back," he said, his voice shaking and his lips stiff from fright.

"I bet you found 'em," Mr. Bertram growled, chomping on his cigar. "I bet you found 'em right where Momma keeps 'em."

Mrs. Bertram's face poked around and under her son's armpit. She stared at Toby, startled. And then her face split into a grin. "The ghosty boy!" she cackled. "An' 'is dog!"

"Momma," Mr. Bertram said, craning his neck to look down at her. "I think we found us the cul-prit.

There's yer radio. Now, Momma, why didn't you tell me your jar of pennies was took too?"

"My pin-nies!" Mrs. Bertram cried. "The ghosty boy found my pin-nies!" She quickly squeezed around her son and ran down the stairs, the huge green bathrobe flapping behind her. "Here!" she said, putting her nose up next to the jar. "All those Indian-headed pin-nies and the steel ones from the war. I knew you'd find 'em." She grinned at Toby like a Halloween pumpkin.

"Give me those, ya little thief!" Mr. Bertram roared, stumbling down the steps. Whiskers bared her teeth. Her growl deepened and her ears flattened against her head. "I should beat the livin' daylights outta ya, stealin' from my momma." He nudged his mother aside and kicked at Whiskers. Whiskers snapped at Mr. Bertram as she skittered out of the way. Mr. Bertram grabbed for the jar of pennies.

Toby panicked. He staggered backward and the radio cord hobbled his feet. Toby's arms shot out and Mr. Bertram lunged, grabbing the radio as it flew upward. The jar smashed against the driveway, scattering pennies and slivers of glass at their feet.

Mr. Bertram yanked and the cord snaked around Toby's ankles, biting into his skin. "I didn't steal 'em!" Toby screeched, struggling for balance, tears blobbing down his face. "I just brought 'em back, just like you wanted!" Whiskers retreated with Toby, her teeth showing, her head down, and her hackles up.

"You little liar," Mr. Bertram growled.

"Oooh," Mrs. Bertram moaned. Mr. Bertram turned toward his mother, who was kneeling on the driveway and holding up a hand. Blood ran down her pointing finger, across her hand, and down her forearm. It reached her elbow and gathered into a large drop that broke away and splattered onto the driveway.

"Momma, you git up from there!" Mr. Bertram said sharply. "There's glass there and now you've gone and cut yourself."

"What's hap-pinning?" Mrs. Bertram moaned, her eyes large and horrified. "The dead don't bleed."

Toby stared. "I'm sorry, Mrs. Bertram," he sobbed.

"I'm bleedin'," Mrs. Bertram moaned. "A miracle! The dead is risen!"

"Now lookee what ya done," Mr. Bertram shouted at Toby, grabbing his mother's arm and pulling her to her feet as if she were a two-year-old.

Toby turned and ran past the garbage cans and down the alley, chased by the thunder of Mr. Bertram's voice. "Don't you never come back here! Never! Never! Never!"

Toby and Whiskers snuck home as dusk glowed, like a television screen just turned off. Toby stood for a moment in the shadows of the porch, listening. He heard his parents talking softly in the kitchen and he smelled leftovers from the school lunch. Toby held the screen door open for Whiskers and followed her inside.

He stood like a stranger in the kitchen doorway,

bathed in light and smells as thick as steam from a hot shower. The chili con carne smelled better in this kitchen than in the kitchen at school—less confused and mixed with the smell of sour milk and children. His mother turned from the stove.

"To-bee!" she smiled. "Yer home!"

His father straightened up from the table, where he had been leaning over arranging silverware on either side of the plates. "Well, well," he said, "al'ays in time fer din-ear. An' he looks hungry too."

Toby looked down at his shoes, stained green around the edges from running through a freshly mown lawn. "Sorry I'm late," he said.

"Naw," his father said, waving a spoon at him and smiling. "Go git worshed up."

He looked up shyly and watched his mother totter toward the table as she carried a steaming pan with both hands, her jaw set in concentration as she leaned back on her heels. "G'wan! G'wan!" she gasped. She strained to look at him down her nose and the pan tipped back and forth with each step.

A smile pushed on the inside of Toby's mouth, but didn't quite break through. He turned around and walked through his parents' bedroom to the bathroom. He felt old and tired. He looked into the mirror above the sink, expecting to see his face withered and drawn. Instead, Toby saw his own pinched face, dirt smudged on his chin where he had slapped at a mosquito and his long eyelashes bleached white. Toby looked at his hair, arranged on his head like the haystacks on his grandfather's farm—yellow at the crown and turning darker on the thatched sides.

Toby quickly washed his hands and rubbed his face on the damp towel where he dried his hands. He rubbed hard and his face tingled.

As Toby walked into the kitchen, Whiskers turned her head to watch from where she sat next to his chair. His father's hand covered his mother's on the space between their plates. Toby sat down.

"Hep yerself," his father said, patting his mother's hand before reaching for the pot. "How was school?" He handed the pot to Toby. "Doin' good in yer figgers?"

The smile pushed out and Toby nodded, looking at his father's face and glancing shyly at his mother. He held the pot for his mother as she helped herself and they ate in comfortable silence.

Toby stared at his empty plate, trying to decide if the smears of chili looked like a face or not. "To-bee." He looked up at his mother. "To-bee, I haf a sir-prize fo' you." He followed as she shuffled to the living room and picked up a book that was lying on top of the television. "Miz Gun-er-son said you my lack to read this . . . out loud! To us!" She held the book out to Toby. He took it and looked at the cover: three alert animals, two dogs and a cat, were looking at something or someone in the woods off the cover.

"What's it called?" his father asked, sitting on one

end of the sofa. He looked at Toby and patted the cushion next to him.

"The Incredible Journey," Toby said slowly, opening the book. The binding was stiff and cracked.

Air in the sofa's cushion whooshed out as Toby's mother sat at the other end of the couch. Whiskers lay down between their feet. She rested her head on her paws, which were crossed very ladylike, and kept her eyes on him.

Toby stepped over Whiskers and squeezed between his parents on the middle cushion. The sofa sagged in the middle, causing his parents to lean toward him. Toby held the book in his lap tightly to keep his hands from shaking. He could almost feel the energy of the three animals squeezing from the pages of the book. His father's arm settled on the couch behind him, and Toby leaned into the hollow under his father's arm. His father's smell was strong and reassuring. He felt his mother's lively eyes gazing on him and he pictured her determined, crooked smile.

He opened to what looked like the first page. " 'The Beasts,' " he began, his voice rusty. He took a deep breath and followed the words with his pointing finger, sounding out the words he didn't know. " 'I think I could turn and live with animals, they are so placid and self-contain'd. . . .' " Toby's voice picked up strength as he read, and the words hung in the air as fragrant as dinner, feeding their imaginations.

Toby looked up into his father's face. A tear was

sneaking down the high ridge of his father's cheek. His father smiled weakly and nodded. "Go-wan, Toby. Go-wan. It's . . . perty—hearin' you read."

Toby's chest puffed out to make room for his pride. He read in a voice that he'd never used before—more sure, even on the words he didn't know. " 'I stand and look at them long and long. They do not sweat and whine about their condition. They do not lie awake in the dark and weep for their sins. . . .' "

His mother touched his arm and pointed to Whiskers on the floor. "E'en Wis-skers lakes you t'read."

Toby followed his mother's finger. Whiskers's head was raised and tipped to one side. Her ears were cocked forward. She studied Toby as if she were seeing him for the first time. Toby laughed and rubbed the side of her neck with the tip of his shoe. "She never heard me read before!" he said, looking at his mother. She beamed.

"Me neither," she said. She tapped the book with her hand. "G'wan, To-bee. We're a-liss-nin'."

Toby read until his voice faded and his father's head began to nod and his mother's breathing became low and regular.

" '. . . neither moved from his side,' " he read, almost in a whisper, before he closed the book.

10

Toby smelled something funny as he sat at his desk. He looked down at his pants and saw nothing telltale. He'd changed his underwear yesterday and he'd worn his jeans only a couple of days. He looked at the bottoms of his shoes. He hadn't stepped in any dog poop walking to school. But that's what it smelled like.

Other kids were settling into their seats, talking and shuffling, yawning and wiggling their rears, kneading them into numbness, making the desks squeak. Harold was perched on Robin's desk top listening to her, one foot on the floor and the other leg dangling. Harold glanced at Toby, his eyes connecting with Toby's for an instant, and then snapped back to Robin.

The bell rang and Harold slipped off Robin's desk and sauntered to his own. He slid into the seat and slouched, his legs straddling the desk in front of him. Harold crossed his arms on his stomach and stared straight ahead.

The funny smell bothered Toby. He glanced again at his feet to make sure he hadn't stepped in anything. Robin twisted around in her seat and sniffed quizzically. Toby shrugged his shoulders and she smiled before she turned around. Toby liked her smile.

Miss Follensby strode to the front of the class and stood, looking stern, silently demanding attention. She scanned the classroom as several kids remained turned in their seats, talking. Her stern look became angry and her nostrils pinched together, causing her mouth to lift into a faint snarl.

Loudly, Miss Follensby cleared her throat. Talking stopped and desks creaked as kids faced the front of the classroom.

"That's better," she said, her chest drooping in relief. "You know I don't like to raise my voice and you know that I like to start the day on a good note." She stepped to the chalkboard and grabbed a piece of chalk. Looking over her shoulder at the class and writing on the chalkboard at the same time, she said, "I want to start the morning with a little surprise." Her voice was cheery but her eyes were wary.

Her writing sloped downward on the chalkboard and

her letters grew smaller and crowded. Toby squinted and read: "If I could be anything . . ."

"We are going to start a unit this afternoon on careers. And I want you to spend a little time now thinking about what you would like to be when you grow up." Miss Follensby put the chalk and eraser in the tray and put her hands on her hips. "When I was your age, I already knew that I wanted to be a teacher." Her smile was thin. "And I think I made the right choice."

She scanned the class. "I will give you ten minutes to put some thoughts on paper. During the day I'd like for you to think about what you would like to do when you grow up and to add to your thoughts."

Toby opened his desk top. He reached for a pencil and his hand stopped in midair. On top of his reading book sat a plastic sandwich bag with the mouth folded back. Toby looked closer at the plastic bag and saw that it held a pile of dog poop. The smell was strong and Toby quickly closed his desk top. He stared at the back of Harold's head. As he stared Harold's hand reached up, the middle finger extended and alone, and scratched the back of his head. Before he brought his hand back down, Harold wagged the finger back and forth in Toby's direction.

"Toby?" Toby's back jerked up straight. He looked up at Miss Follensby through his eyelashes. "Toby, are you going to write down some thoughts about what you want to be when you grow up?" she asked slowly, her patience barely showing. Toby looked back down at his desk top.

"What *is* that smell?" Miss Follensby asked. She tipped her head and looked down at Toby's feet. "Perhaps you stepped in something. Toby, go to the boys' room and clean off your shoes, please. And hurry. I would like for you to get some ideas down on paper." Miss Follensby wove the fingers of her hands together in front of her and continued to walk down the aisle.

Holding his breath Toby quickly reached inside his desk and grabbed the top of the sandwich bag. Crumping the top of it closed in his fist he pulled it out of his desk. A shudder passed through his arm as he thought of what he was feeling through the thin plastic. The loose softness of the bag's contents were too large to squeeze into the pocket of his jeans. So Toby covered the bag with both hands and held it against himself, as if his stomach hurt. He got up from his desk and rushed out of the classroom and into the hall.

Toby ran to the toilet, which was still exposed as a throne in the bathroom. He flushed the bag down and washed his hands three times to get rid of the smell. Back in the classroom he opened his desk top to find a piece of paper and a pencil. Next to his reading book he noticed a scrap of paper covered with spidery handwriting. "Need to change your diapers?" it asked.

At recess, Toby stayed near the school doors, close to Mrs. Schell. He kept an eye on Harold, John, and Pete, who were talking to Robin and some of her friends near the swings.

The recess dragged on and, like first-graders on the monkey bars, Toby's head tumbled with ideas for getting even with Harold for putting such a nasty thing in his desk. Toby closed his eyes and pictured himself standing over Harold, who was bound with ropes and gagged with some dirty underwear and lying helplessly on the railroad tracks. Harold's head rested on one rail and his legs lay over the other. Toby felt the air grow nervous as the train approached. He watched Harold's eyes grow crazy with fear.

Toby shuddered. He kept his eyes closed and turned around, trying to think of something else. He was stalking through a forest, a shotgun nestled into the crook of one arm. He strained to listen and heard a rustle and crash in front of him. He saw Harold dart behind a tree. Toby crouched and walked silently toward the tree. Harold jumped out and scampered away, shreds of clothes flapping where they had been torn by branches and thorns. Toby followed—steadily, grimly, silently—until he saw Harold collapse in a crying heap on the forest floor, curled up like a baby and holding his head in his hands. Toby walked up and shouldered the gun. He held his breath as he looked down the blue-black of the barrel spine and squinted one eye for aiming. . . .

Toby opened his eyes and blinked away the sharp sunlight. He looked down at the soothing dark gray of the asphalt. A little yellow butterfly landed near Toby's feet and he knelt to look at it.

The butterfly's wings were frayed and tattered and they opened and closed and opened and closed slightly— like breathing. He stuck out his finger and gently nudged its feet, trying to make it walk onto his finger and roost like a bird. With a burst of energy the butterfly took off. Toby followed its rise, the wind pushing it sideways, and found himself looking at Harold and John and Pete, who stood just a few feet away.

"Howdy, old buddy," Harold said, his voice loud and friendly. "How ya doin'?" He walked over to Toby, grabbed him under his armpit, and pulled him up. "Let's go see if we can find that butterfly."

Toby looked over at Mrs. Schell. She was smiling at them. She probably thinks they're nice for paying attention to me, Toby thought. Harold turned and smiled at her. "Hi, Mrs. Schell," he called, giving her a little wave with his other hand. When he turned around, his smile was gone and his eyes were hard.

Harold let go of Toby's armpit and threw his arm over Toby's shoulder, drawing him close. "Let's go over there," he said, nodding toward the schoolyard fence.

"Sure thing," John said. "Lots of butterflies over there." He giggled. "Butterfly!" he called in falsetto. "Butterfly! Come here, butterfly!" His shoulders shook as he silently laughed at his own joke.

"Come on," Pete muttered. "We got better things to do."

"I don't think so," Harold said, looking over his

shoulder at Pete. "My dad told me something last night you two should know about. Something to do with our good friend Toby here." He bent his arm, squeezing Toby's neck in its crook.

"Yeah?" John asked. A big smile spread across his face. "You found out his dad is part dog?"

Toby tensed. With a jerk he spun around under Harold's arm. He faced John, his hands fisted. He dropped his chin and glared through his eyelashes.

"Hey, wait just a minute," Harold said, grabbing a back pocket of Toby's jeans and jerking. He looked up at John. "Shut up. I got something to say to this little pisser." He jerked again at Toby's pants. "Turn around, re-turd. I want to make sure you understand."

"Hey, I didn't mean nothin'," John said, smirking and holding both hands up. He sidled up next to Harold. Toby turned, following him, ready to strike out. Harold's hand slipped out of his pocket. "Just something I heard from a bitch named Whiskers."

"Shut up!" Harold said impatiently. He glared at John. Looking back at Toby he said. "My old man told us last night at dinner that he was as proud as he could be . . . of you. He said he got a call from Mr. Bertram yesterday and Mr. Bertram said that you returned that radio you stole from his mother. And that you returned something else too—a jar of pennies." Harold looked over to register the surprised look on John's face.

"Oh, shit," Pete said, softly, walking around Toby to Harold's other side. "That means Toby's been to our secret hiding place. He knows."

Harold's eyes flashed at Pete. "Aren't you smart!" he snapped. Harold looked back at Toby. "Where did you get that radio, Toby? And those pennies? Come on. We want to hear you tell us where you got that stuff." His voice was singsong and he took a step closer to Toby.

Toby glared at Harold, his breath coming in short, rapid bursts.

Harold glanced over Toby's shoulder. "Old biddy," he muttered, smiling and waving. "Mrs. Schell's worried about you, Toby," he said, looking back at Toby, his smile disappearing. "And so am I. If you don't mind your own business and stay away from the church cellar, terrible things could happen to you. And I mean terrible. Worse than dog shit in your desk. Much worse. That dog of yours, for example, could end up hanging by its tail from a tree . . . or by its neck. Know what I mean?"

Toby looked Harold straight in the eyes, zapping him with all the hate in his body. The bell rang and kids scurried into the school like ants into an anthole.

"Just remember," Harold said, poking Toby in the shoulder with each word, "or that dog is a goner." He spit down at Toby's feet and swaggered off, his hands in his pockets.

"Butterfly! Butterfly!" Toby heard John call. And then Toby heard them laugh.

Toby opened his locker door gingerly and slipped his corrected papers for the day on top of the teetering pile that was now level with his chin. He shut the door quickly before the pile lost its balance and fell out.

As he walked toward the double doors he heard footsteps running after him from behind. Instinctively, preparing for an ambush, he hunched his shoulders and slunk against the wall.

"Toby." He heard Robin's voice and looked up in surprise. "Hi." She almost sounded shy.

Robin opened a door for him as they walked outside. Toby swallowed and nodded his thanks as he stepped into the sweet air. He looked around quickly, hoping that Harold wasn't watching him walk with Robin.

"Don't worry," Robin said. "Harold took off faster than a . . . greased pig."

Toby's shoulders relaxed, but his eyes continued to roam to the right and left.

"I really miss New Jersey," Robin said, looking up at the sky and taking a deep breath. "The air even smells . . . different here. You know, I wish sometimes I could go back and stay with my sister in Teaneck. We used to go to the movies together—just the two of us. And she would take me to the R-rated ones and tell the lady at the ticket window she was my mother." Robin sighed.

"We have a movie house," Toby said quietly. He looked up at Robin's face to see if she had heard him.

"It's not the same," she said. "All the movies are old."

"Oh," Toby said. Robin turned down a street leading away from his house. He followed alongside her anyway.

"Ever been to Jersey?" she asked, frowning down on him.

"No," Toby said.

"You sure?" Robin studied his face. Toby looked down at his feet in embarrassment.

"I asked Harold," Robin said, "and he . . . laughed. He said you've never been outside this . . . county before. But I just had to ask you."

"Why?" Toby looked back up at her.

"You remind me of a kid who lived up the street from me back in Jersey . . . when I was little. Everything about you makes me think of him. Even the way you walk and . . . You know, everybody tries to act so smart when they're all such . . . babies." She looked down at Toby. "You're just like that kid. . . . You're the only person around who's smarter than you let on. The way you act dumb until . . . the time is just right." She giggled. "That spitball was . . . perfect. Even if I'd thought of that I wouldn't have been able to hit Harold on the neck in a . . . million years."

Toby felt the tips of his ears heat up.

"He moved away and I didn't think of him again—until I saw you. I just can't remember his name," Robin continued. "I thought it was Tom or . . . Terry or . . . I even thought it could be Toby. But you never lived in New Jersey?"

Toby shook his head.

"People would pick on him," Robin said, looking up into the sky. "But if anybody *really* hurt him . . ."—she swung a fist up underneath Toby's nose and smiled—

". . . I decked 'em." She looked back down at him. "He and I were real . . . close."

Robin stopped and faced Toby. "My house is down . . . there." She tipped her head over her left shoulder. She turned around and walked away. "See you later," she called over her shoulder.

Toby puzzled over what Robin had said as he back-tracked home. Could there be a person somewhere that looked and acted like he did? Was there somebody out there who felt the same way he did inside, like a real version of the person he saw in the bathroom mirror? Toby didn't know if he liked that idea or not.

As he passed by the school for the second time, Toby decided to go home by way of the railroad tracks. He turned into an alley, snuck through a backyard, and disappeared into the thick bushes that guarded the tracks. He peered up and down the tracks to make sure he was alone before he stepped out of the bushes and onto the cinders. If a train comes, he told himself, stepping with stiff legs from tie to tie, I won't get out of the way. I'll just let it run me down and smash me like a penny on a rail—flat and stretched out and so smooth it doesn't look like a penny. When they find me, maybe they'll think it was a dog or skunk or cat or something, he thought.

Toby took his time, daring a train to come roaring down the track. But no train came. And when Toby turned off into a backyard, his insides relaxed and his breathing came easier.

He walked up the sidewalk to his house and lifted

his eyes to the porch, expecting to see Whiskers waiting for him. The porch was empty. Toby walked around to the side of the porch and, dropping to his hands and knees, he peered underneath into the cool darkness.

"Whiskers?" he asked quietly. He heard nothing and stood up, wiping his dusty hands on his pants.

Toby remembered Harold's threat and was seized by a horrible fear that something terrible had happened to Whiskers. *Maybe they got her while Robin was talking to me. Was Robin helping Harold by walking with me?* He pictured Whiskers hanging from a tree—her hind legs pointing up, her body curling, her tail straining back and forth—trying to loosen the rope around her neck. Toby closed his eyes and, as hard as he could, struck the top of his head with the flat of his hand. The image exploded into darkness and was gone. Shaken, he slowly opened his eyes.

"No. No. No," he muttered, rubbing the spot where he'd hit himself. "Whiskers is all right. Whiskers?" he pleaded quietly. "Whiskers? Whiskers!" he called, panic bleeding through his voice like blood through a bandage. "Whiskers!"

Toby searched frantically in all directions—up and down and around the porch—and he dropped to his hands and knees to search under the bushes that ran along the house. He turned on all fours toward the Bertrams' house. Dark puddles of oil marked where Mr. Bertram's car had been. Toby scrambled upright and lurched toward the backyard. "Whiskers!" he yelled.

His head snapped left when he saw the screen door

to the Bertrams' kitchen door ajar. Maybe she went in there, he thought, running toward their house. He kicked the screen door open farther and rushed inside the open kitchen door.

Pots and pans were strewn across the floor. The kitchen table was pushed up against the refrigerator, and the kitchen chairs were scattered around like bodies with knees drawn up to their chests.

"Mrs. Bertram!" Toby called, running into the living room. "Whiskers!" The living room looked untouched except for a lamp knocked over onto the floor. Toby charged up to the couch, landing on the cushions with his knees. He peered behind it and shook the curtains. "Mrs. Bertram!" he yelled, turning around. "Whiskers!"

Toby hopped off the couch and rushed into Mrs. Bertram's bedroom. Framed pictures were lying face-down on top of the dresser and clothes hung out of its opened drawers. Boxes pulled halfway out from under her bed were opened and had been rifled. The radio Toby had brought back was still on the nightstand by her bed. But pennies were scattered over her bedspread.

"Mrs. Bertram!" Toby shrieked. "Whiskers!"

He stood, stunned, in the middle of the room. *Harold and John and Pete did this?* Toby could hardly believe it. *Where is Mrs. Bertram? Where is Whiskers?*

Toby spun around and raced through the house, leaping over a chair in the kitchen and flying off the steps. He ran across the yard and down the alley toward the church.

I'll rescue them. His legs moved faster than they'd ever moved before, barely touching the ground. His throat and lungs burned and his head felt lighter and lighter, like a helium balloon let go into the air. The ground tilted and light and sound faded. He felt as though he were going to faint. Toby staggered up to a fence and grabbed a picket just as his legs buckled. He closed his eyes and the sound of his heavy breathing slowly returned.

I've got to rescue them, he thought, as he opened his eyes and straightened his legs. His ears tingled. Faintly he heard the sound of barking toward the creek. He held his breath and listened harder. It was Whiskers.

Toby's heart sprang ahead of him as he pushed off the picket and ran between two houses toward the creek.

The barking grew louder, persistent, and Toby plowed through the tangled underbrush of the woods, holding his forearms crossed in front of his face to keep branches and leaves from cutting his eyes and mouth. Branches poked his stomach and whipped at his legs. "I'm coming!" he called. The barking became a happy *welp*.

Toby broke through the woods and stood, teetering, on the high bank cut by the river. He grabbed a branch to steady himself and strained to hear, upriver and downriver. To his left he heard a high-pitched cackle— Mrs. Bertram!

He scrambled along the bank and called out, "Mrs. Bertram! Mrs. Bertram! It's me! Toby!" Whiskers bounded through the bushes, her tail high, her tongue lolling from the side of her mouth. She reared up and her paws struck Toby on the chest. He tumbled backward. Whiskers's tail beat back and forth as she licked Toby's face.

"Cut it out," Toby said, sitting up. He scrambled to his feet. "Come on," he cried, running toward Mrs. Bertram's garbled voice.

Mrs. Bertram, dressed in the huge green bathrobe, was parting some bushes clinging to the lip of the riverbank, peering down and muttering. "Harold," Toby heard. "Come outta there. You ain't s'posed ta be skinny-dippin' in the river. Come on. Come on out and git'cher clothes on."

Toby walked up quietly, as if she were a wild animal easily spooked. "Mrs. Bertram," he said softly. "Mrs. Bertram, it's me, Toby."

"Shh," Mrs. Bertram hissed, a finger to her lips. "Don't scare 'em. Look at 'em all nakey. They better be careful, jumpin' off that ol' branch, that they don't go and hit their heads on a rock or log or sump-in'."

She turned to Toby and gazed at him. For the first time Toby looked into her eyes and was afraid. He wasn't afraid that she would hurt him. He was afraid that she was crazy crazy—that she might think she could fly and would jump off the bank and break her own neck.

Carefully, not making a sound, Toby crept toward Mrs. Bertram, his hand extended. Whiskers whimpered behind him. "Mrs. Bertram, it's time to go home," he said. Slowly, slowly, slowly, his hand grasped her arm. He tightened his grip and felt nothing but terry cloth until his hand encircled the bone of her upper arm. "Come on," he coaxed. And he pulled her away from the bank.

"The ghosty boy!" she exclaimed, as if seeing him for the first time. "An' his doggie! Oh, let's go on home an' have us some bug juice! Nasty, nasty poltergeists. I hope they left us some bug juice." She turned toward the river. "Bye-bye," she cooed, lifting her other hand and waving.

As Toby carefully guided Mrs. Bertram through the woods, he listened to her babble. At first what she said didn't make any sense. She talked about skinny-dipping and pennies and poltergeists and her kitchen all in the same breath. Toby pictured chairs skinny-dipping and pennies twitching like Mexican jumping beans. But as she talked other images flashed in Toby's head—and the faces in these images were of Harold and John and Pete. Slowly, Toby connected these images like pieces of a torn photograph, and a moving collage grew inside Toby's head. Harold and John and Pete had come to call on Mrs. Bertram. They'd dragged Whiskers with them. Mrs. Bertram had fought the boys off by throwing pots and pans at them and chasing them around the house with her broom. She'd chased them into her bedroom and John wrestled her to the bed and sat on top of her while Harold and Pete ransacked her room.

"They were a-lookin' fer somethin'," Mrs. Bertram whispered mysteriously. "An' they didn't know where it was. Tad almost told 'em. But I swatted that momma's boy in the face and pushed 'im off a me and chased all of 'em outta the house." She chuckled. "Woulda got 'em too, 'cept my bathrobe tangled up my legs. But I outsmarted them little buggers," she whispered. She ducked her head and Toby ducked too before he realized that there was nothing to avoid. "I knew whar they were headed. Off to the swimmin' hole. An' I follered."

Her bathrobe was coming undone, showing the flat, freckled folds of her chest. As they came out of the woods, Toby stepped in front of her. She stood patiently while he pulled the robe closed like a curtain and tightened the belt. She slipped her arm through his and they walked arm in arm down one block and up another. She talked on while Toby escorted her down the sidewalk, feeling confused and angry and scared.

Toby led her up the kitchen steps and inside. "Oh lookee," she sagged. Quickly, Toby grabbed a chair and slipped it under her before she fell, bottom first, to the floor. "What a mess," she sighed.

"I'll help clean up," Toby offered, kneeling beside Whiskers and holding her close. She was shaking—from fear or happiness, Toby didn't know which. "Want some bug juice?"

"Hep yerself. It's in the 'frigerator," Mrs. Bertram sighed, waving her hand toward the sink.

Toby stood and walked to the refrigerator. He pulled the table out and opened the door. He reached for a jar of purple juice and opened the lid. He sniffed.

Fumes filled his head, withering his nose. He walked to the cupboards and pulled down a glass, filled it, and walked over to Mrs. Bertram.

"Here," he said, handing the glass to her. Mrs. Bertram nodded like a child falling asleep while sitting up, and raised the glass to within an inch of her lips.

"An' Harold was sech a good-lookin' boy," she muttered before taking a sip.

11

Toby put the kitchen in order, working around Mrs. Bertram and twice refilling her glass with bug juice. She sat in a daze, her eyes half closed. Her lower lip stuck out in a tired pout. Her head nodded slightly—as if she were agreeing with a voice talking inside her head.

Toby picked up the last chair from the floor and set it on its feet. He looked at the side of Mrs. Bertram's face. The skin under her chin hung like a sack of marbles. And even her nose had tiny wrinkles crisscrossing it. Her head jerked up and her eyes flew open. "Bein' dead's not so different from bein' alive," she exclaimed. Her eyelids fluttered a moment and then slowly settled like a shade half-drawn and swaying in a gentle breeze. Toby glanced around the kitchen. It looked orderly—except for Mrs. Bertram, who was sitting over a spot of worn-through linoleum facing a corner of the kitchen. She looked a little like a doll dragged by her feet through the yard. Her head swiveled toward him. Only white showed from below her half-closed eyes. "Poor little ghosty boy. And what did th' preacher do ta ya, anyhow?"

Toby sighed. I don't know, he thought.

He stood up and Whiskers got to her feet. "Let's go pick up your bedroom," he said, holding out a hand to help Mrs. Bertram up. She opened her eyes wide, put the glass into his hand, and lurched upright. Wobbling, she made for the living room.

"Wish I was invisible," she muttered. "Most ghosts are invisible. That's how it should be. Bein' seen gives me a headache."

Toby set the glass on the table and followed Mrs. Bertram into her bedroom. She stopped and grabbed the sides of her head. Swaying back and forth, as if she were trying to unscrew her head from her shoulders, she moaned softly. "Lookee that. My pin-nies is all over. An' ma boxes is a mess," she said, letting go of her head and stumbling toward the bed. She belly flopped onto the bed and herded pennies into a pile by sweeping her arms and hands over the rumpled bedspread as if she were swimming. "An' this a'one has a Indian on it. An' this 'un too. An' this 'un. Got me a tribe of pin-nies, jes' waitin' fer a powwow." She chuckled and kicked up her feet behind her.

Toby walked around the bed to the dresser. He stuffed clothes into the drawers before closing them. As he set the photographs back on their stands, he studied the faces and people caught in the frames. In one, Mrs. Bertram stood in the dark crevice between a hulking man and a large, awkward boy. Her jet black hair was pulled back and her jaw stuck out at a jaunty angle— the same as now. Her arms hooked around thick arms hanging on either side of her, as if to keep the frowning man and sheepish boy from leaving. The man looked like an older, grumpier version of Mr. Bertram. That must have been her husband, Toby thought. The boy was pudgy and his long pants were too short, exposing the tops of his socks and part of his shins, as white as the socks. His white T-shirt was tattooed with food stains.

Toby picked up another picture, so badly faded that the images looked like bruises. He searched for clues that the bride was Mrs. Bertram. The bride's mouth and eyes were fixed in a cloud of dark hair. The groom stared defiantly into the camera, looking angry.

Toby didn't notice Mrs. Bertram walking up beside him. He jumped when she spoke. "Ol' Harry," she said quietly, holding onto Toby's shoulder with both hands and leaning. "Didn't want ta git married. But George was on the way. A wild oat sprouted inside a me." She smiled at Toby and patted her tummy with one hand.

"Claimed I trapped 'im." She let go of Toby's shoulder and tottered toward the closet. "Woulda rather trapped a porky-pine, tell the truth. Haven't seen him since I passed on. 'Spect he's burnin' in hell an' can't get out fer a visit."

Toby looked at the photograph more closely. He'd seen Mrs. Bertram's young face before . . . someplace . . . framed in ivy. . . .

Toby sucked in his breath. He'd seen Mrs. Bertram's young face in the brooch that Robin had worn. The one Harold gave her. The face in the photograph began to nod in agreement, but Toby looked down and saw that his hands were shaking up and down. He tensed his arms to make them still and carefully placed the photograph back onto the dresser. He breathed deeply and smelled the baby-powder scent of Mrs. Bertram right behind him.

The roar of an engine shattered the silence as a car charged up the driveway. Toby spun toward the round alarm clock sitting on a nightstand by the bed. Its hands were covering the six like a fat boy caught naked. It's too early for Mr. Bertram to be home, Toby thought, panicking. He turned from the dresser and saw Whiskers bristle. A car door slammed shut. The kitchen's screen door banged open and Toby heard Mr. Bertram bellow, "Momma, I'm home. Momma, let's go out and get us somethin' nice ta eat." The voice grew louder, each word punctuated by a heavy footfall. "Let's celebrate my gettin' fired from that flea baggy . . ."

Mr. Bertram stepped into the doorway and his jaw dropped. His cigar stub drooped and was about to fall off his lower lip when his mouth clamped shut like a spring trap. Mrs. Bertram turned around and eyed her son from the closet, annoyed. "Fired?" she asked, crossing her arms over her chest. "You got fired . . . agin?"

"What the hell are you doin' here?" Mr. Bertram yelled, staring pop-eyed at Toby. Red crept up his neck and face and bled into his hair. "For Chrissake, I tol'ja I'd skin ya alive if I ever caught ya in here agin! An' what's this?" He looked like a grown-up version of the kid in the photo—busting to cry. He ran, tripping, to the boxes pulled out from the bed. He looked up at Toby, the flab around his jaw quivering. "I'm a-gonna kill you!" He trembled and started to scramble around the bed.

Quickly Mrs. Bertram stepped in front of Toby and Whiskers. Mr. Bertram stopped and leaned back to keep his belly from bumping her. "This ghosty boy is a-heppin'. Been visited by those nasty poltergeists and he's a-heppin' me clean up. Ya hear?" Her voice crackled like electricity and Mr. Bertram stepped back, startled.

His eyes slowly hardened as he rolled his cigar stump around in his mouth. He sneered at Toby. "Heppin' clean you out, I'd say," he said, the fire returning to his face. "Takin' advantage of a woman gone crazy. Thought I'd niver think of you since you brought back the last stuff you stole, didn't 'cha." He stepped closer and tried to ease his mother aside. Whiskers growled and Toby felt blood drain from his face.

"Now lookee here, young man," Mrs. Bertram said. She walked into her son's belly, her chin stuck out so that the hairs on the end of it almost touched his chest. She unfolded her arms and shook a bony finger in his face. "I'll take you over my knee and wallop you 'til you cain't cry no more. You leave this ghosty boy alone!"

"Momma . . ." Mr. Bertram said, tightening his grip on her shoulder.

Toby felt a hot gush of fear and anger grow in the pit of his stomach and burn upward. He swallowed, gagged, and his shoulders twitched forward. He opened his mouth and words pushed out, hot and thick as vomit. "I didn't do nothin' but clean up! I've *never* done nothin' to you . . . you . . . you wild oat!"

Mr. Bertram grabbed at Toby. "Now, George," Mrs. Bertram warned, striking his arm down.

Toby closed his eyes, ducked his head, and charged toward the bedroom door. Whiskers tucked her tail and scampered at his feet.

"Wha' . . ." Mr. Bertram blurted. "Come back here, ya little pre-vert!"

Toby ran, arms flailing, through the living room. The walls seemed to vibrate with the pounding of Mr. Bertram's feet. Toby dropped his head farther and charged through the kitchen, kicking open the screen door with his feet an instant before his head would have smashed into it. He flew down the stairs and across the backyard and down the alley. Air whizzed by his ears and he felt like a bullet screaming through space, aimed for the Prairieview Lutheran Church cellar doors.

Toby felt stronger than he'd ever felt. He sucked in air, his relaxed lower lip drawn in and out with the force of his breathing. He leaned forward, his legs shoving off each step like a sprinter pushing off a starting block. He cut around a fence like a jet cutting around the cap of a thunderhead and flew across the church lawn up to the cellar doors.

He bent down and grabbed a door by its corner and, straightening his legs, he flung it open with a grunt. He looked down the steps into the dim and flickering light. He heard a frantic whisper, "Get the light." And the dim light blinked and then blackened.

Toby looked at Whiskers, who was standing behind him. "Come on," he panted, stepping toward the stairs. Whiskers sat, her ears flopped back and her tongue hanging off to one side. "Come on," he insisted, patting his knee. But Whiskers turned her head toward the side, avoiding Toby's eyes, and didn't move. Toby turned and walked carefully down the stairs.

He stood for a moment at the bottom, letting his eyes adjust to the dark and catching his breath. When his blinks were darker than the room and his breathing more relaxed, he walked toward the opening in the box wall. He heard nervous whispering and rustlings.

Taking a deep breath, and smelling cigarette smoke, Toby plunged into the hiding place.

In the quiet, Toby heard his heart beating. The air

was thick, making Toby feel that he was breathing polluted water. He took a tentative step backward, peering ahead, trying to locate Harold and John and Pete by sound or smell or sight. But the heavy smoke dulled his senses.

Toby jumped as somebody moved to his right. "She-it," Harold's voice hissed from the darkness. "It's only the re-turd." Toby looked toward the voice and saw Harold's dark shape slump against the box wall.

Three more dark shapes slipped silently toward Harold and Toby was seized by an urge to flee. One shape began to cough as if it had swallowed wrong. Toby jumped but he remembered Mrs. Bertram's room and Mr. Bertram's anger and he clenched his hands into fists and tried to anchor himself to the ground by curling his toes tightly in his shoes. The coughing stopped.

"Why'ja do it?" Toby asked, his voice squeaky as a cricket's. He stared at Harold's shape, which was growing clearer in the darkness. "Why don't 'cha leave us alone?" His voice now sounded like the yowl of a cat.

"What's it to ya?" Harold taunted. He stepped forward and the oval of his face appeared like an almost full moon behind thin night clouds.

Toby stared at the dark shadows below Harold's forehead but didn't see Harold's eyes. The shadows made Harold's head look like a skull. "Mr. Bertram thinks *I* did it." Toby's throat tightened.

"Well, now. Isn't that a shame." John's voice leered behind Harold in the darkness.

"Toby," Harold said, a forced friendliness in his voice. "What did I say to you the other day about our hiding place? Do you remember? Didn't I tell you that bad things could happen to you if you came here again? Didn't I say something about your dog?" The voice came nearer and Toby felt air moving. He stepped back.

"He was busy chasing butterflies and didn't hear," John's voice taunted. "Butterfly! Butterfly!" he sang in a high-pitched giggle.

"Toby, this is serious. I hope you understand that we don't take this lightly. We don't like hurting you, but you seem to want us to hurt you, bad. Toby . . ."

"That's . . . enough, Harold." Surprised, Toby peered past Harold toward Robin's voice.

Footsteps strode overhead and the floor above them creaked. Everybody looked up. Toby knew whose footsteps those were. They were the same ones he often heard when he was under the porch at home. He pictured Reverend Olsen's stride—left, right, left, right— his neck stiff in his starched clerical collar, his head facing straight ahead, his black, rubber-heeled shoes biting into the polished wooden floor above.

Toby closed his eyes and pictured footsteps glowing above him while he lay curled under the porch, like a baby inside his mother. He loved that peaceful, warm feeling of security, being hugged by darkness and bathed in love. Suddenly, as he pictured himself curled under the porch, he felt a stranger stirring inside him. Hurt and anger and anguish seared through his body and his back arched and his legs straightened, quivering and tense. Confusion squeezed his head and his shoulders. He tried to move but his arms were pinned along either side of his chest. He felt himself being forced from the warm, safe, quiet place inside his mother—pushed and squeezed—and his lungs burned with the aching need for air. He closed his eyes fiercely to shut out the pain. But the pain flashed white as his head punched through the tight darkness into bright light and noise. His mouth gaped with the shock of cold air in his lungs and on his skin. A wail like that of a newborn baby erupted from deep within him. His head flopped back as the cry swelled from his gut—anguished and pure, terrified and mournful.

"Stop that!" Harold hissed, charging toward Toby and knocking him down. Toby felt Harold's hands groping along his body, searching upwards. Again, Toby's cry split the air like the cry of a wild thing facing death or a baby facing life. The cry was cut short as Harold's hand slammed over Toby's mouth.

Toby wrenched his head free. Harold's hand closed around his mouth again and Toby bit into the soft flesh below Harold's little finger. His lower teeth felt bone and he tasted blood. "Ow!" Harold yelped, yanking his hand away.

"Let's get out of here!" Harold groaned through clenched teeth. He jammed his knee into Toby's side and pushed down to get to his feet. Quick as a cat, Toby sat upright. He grabbed Harold's leg and hugged it to his chest. Harold struggled to escape, shaking his leg and trying to dig the toe of his foot into Toby's taut belly and under his ribs. Toby held tighter and bit into the jeans covering the back of Harold's knee.

"Ow!" Harold cried, falling to the floor.

Toby felt hands grab his shoulders and yank. The jeans slipped through his teeth and his mouth chomped shut, jarring his head. Harold clawed at the dirt, crawling away, through the opening to the hiding place. He fell on his face as Toby lost his grip and Harold's leg slipped through his arms, throwing Harold forward.

A naked bulb dangling above them flashed on and Reverend Olsen clattered down the stairs, puffing, his face twitching with terror.

He stopped, teetering, at the foot of the stairs and stared at the tangle of boys on the floor. He raised his gaze and stared at Robin. "What is going on here?" he asked breathlessly, opening and closing his mouth like a fish. Without taking his eyes off Robin, he sank, sitting on a stair and wiped his forehead with the back of his hand. "What in heaven's name is going on here? I thought somebody was being killed! I've never heard such a sound before." He shuddered, closing his eyes, and slowly stood up.

Harold picked himself up from the floor and brushed dirt from the front of his pants. He bit his lower lip as he studied his bit hand. His forehead knotted and he shook his hand and wiped a bead of blood onto his shirt. His forehead relaxed as a thought pushed out the pain. He looked up at his father and a smile slowly spread across his face.

"We caught him," Harold said, tipping his head

toward Toby. "We were walking by and saw him open the cellar doors and come down." Harold studied his father a moment. He gathered courage from what he saw and continued. "We waited a few minutes and snuck down to see what was going on."

Toby stared at Harold, unbelieving. Harold looked like he believed what he was saying. Toby looked over to John and Pete and Robin. John was nodding, his eyes big with innocence. Pete was looking down at the floor, tracing a semicircle in the dirt with the tip of his sneaker. Toby's eyes pleaded with Robin. He saw the brooch glinting light back at the dangling bulb.

"And?" Reverend Olsen's voice had regained its composure and resonance.

"And we found him down here . . . *smoking*"—Harold pointed with his thumb over his shoulder toward the hiding place—"with some horrible posters on the wall." Harold feigned disgust and glared at Toby.

Reverend Olsen walked toward Toby. "Toby, remember this: I want to be proud of you. It's always better to admit you're wrong than fight it. Is this true, what Harold says?" he asked gravely. He looked sadly at Toby, waiting for Toby to confess.

"No," Toby said, looking up at Reverend Olsen. He felt small as a bug lying at Reverend Olsen's feet. Reverend Olsen loomed over him, his chin tucked into his clerical collar and anger stretching his mouth to breaking. Toby scrambled to his feet and stood, shaking, in front of Reverend Olsen.

"Toby . . ." Reverend Olsen's voice warned.

"N-n-no!" Toby stammered. "Harold's lying!"

Reverend Olsen looked from Toby to Harold.

"Go see for yourself," Harold said, shrugging.

Reverend Olsen looked back at Toby. "I think I'd better take a look." He stepped around Toby slowly.

Toby watched Reverend Olsen walk to the thin gap between the wall and boxes and pause. He stepped into the hiding place. Toby opened his mouth to protest, but no words came out. He couldn't believe what was happening—how Harold had turned everything around and twisted it.

They heard the ripping of paper and Reverend Olsen reappeared in the doorway, holding the poster out at arm's length. Reverend Olsen had grabbed the poster by the scruff of the rock star's neck and was shaking it. "Where did this come from?" He looked directly at Toby. "These posters reek of Satan worship!" His voice trembled like the poster hanging from his hand. "And the smoke! It's thick as sin!" His chin trembled. "Toby! I demand an explanation!" He took a step forward and Toby saw the same wild-eyed craziness in Reverend Olsen's eyes that he saw in Mrs. Bertram's eyes on the bank of the creek. "I want you to explain yourself. Now!"

Toby stared at Reverend Olsen, not believing what was happening. He turned toward Harold and saw a smile twitching at the corners of his mouth. Next to Harold, John displayed his grin openly. Pete's head was still bowed as he watched his toe. The semicircle was wider and deeper now. Robin's jaw was slack with fear.

The brooch winked every time she sucked in a breath of air. Toby stared again at Reverend Olsen's hardened face.

"That's not mine," Toby said, shaken, looking at the poster.

"Do you mean that this is stolen?" Reverend Olsen shook the poster harder. The rock star still smiled and his eyes remained glazed, as if he were too drugged to notice what was happening to him.

"No!" Toby gulped air.

"The Thurstons don't have enough money to buy things like that," Harold pointed out. Reverend Olsen looked at his son and then back to Toby.

"Toby, this is the last straw. I've never been more sure of anything in my life. You are running wild and I don't want you to be a bad influence on your peers." He looked again at Harold, who stared, unblinking, into his father's eyes.

"No!" Toby cried. "No! *I didn't do anything!*"

He spun around and ran for the cellar stairs.

"Grab him!" Reverend Olsen ordered, dropping the poster and starting toward the stairs. John jumped toward Toby and grabbed Toby's T-shirt.

"No!" Toby yelled, lunging upward. The shirt ripped and Toby catapulted up the stairs as John fell backwards onto his rear, the back of Toby's T-shirt in his hand.

"Come back here!" Toby heard Reverend Olsen yell as he raced across the churchyard and down the alley, Whiskers at his feet. Running like scared rabbits, they dodged into a backyard and swerved between the two houses. Gasping for breath Toby shot behind two parked cars into the street. He ran, swinging his arms higher and higher, toward his house. He thought his heart would explode or his head would burst.

He ran up the sidewalk to his house and around the porch and dove underneath into the cool darkness. Trembling violently, he closed his eyes and curled up into a tight ball.

Everybody's crazy.

Whiskers sniffed at the back of his neck and her tongue darted out to lick the dirt mixed with sweat, now crusting. She moved down between the flaps of T-shirt exposing his back.

I wish I'd never been born.

Toby pressed his knees into his eyes until he saw stars. But tears leaked out anyway and Toby floated away into a world of darkness and sorrow.

Toby cringed as he heard a board above him crack and pop. The knock on the door shook the house and Toby could feel it shake his bones.

"Thurston!" Mr. Bertram bellowed. "Thurston, come out here!"

Toby heard footsteps from inside the house approach the door. He heard the door scrape open. "Yes?" he heard his father ask.

"Thurston, is yer boy Toby home?"

The screen door creaked and Toby heard his father shuffle onto the porch. He pictured his father standing in front of Mr. Bertram, hands in his pockets, trying to be friendly.

"No," he heard his father reply.

"Then where the tarnation is he?" Mr. Bertram yelled.

Toby pictured his father trying to look into Mr. Bertram's face but shying away. "I don't know."

"I found yer brat in my momma's room when I came home. It was a mess." Mr. Bertram's voice was choked with anger. "I jes' got it put back together and I don't know if anything's missin'. But I'll tell ya this, an' you listen good: I've put up with enough of you and that little retarded brat of yours! I won't stan' fer it no more! I'm callin' the police and the state an' anybody else who'll see you and yore'n moved outta here and taken care of proper."

"Mr. Bertram," Toby's father began, "you mus' have the wrong boy. Toby's no . . ."

"I SAW HIM!" Mr. Bertram bellowed. "YOU CALLIN' ME A LIAR?"

Toby heard the steps groan as somebody else walked up onto the porch.

"Bertram," he heard Reverend Olsen say. "I could hear you all the way to the church. Let's not disturb the entire neighborhood."

"Listen, Olsen, that Toby broke into my house . . . agin!" Mr. Bertram yelled, boards squeaking as weight shifted on the porch.

"Again?" Reverend Olsen asked, his voice tired. "Well, now. I just came from the church, where my son and his friends caught Toby in the church cellar smoking, surrounded by posters of Satan worshippers." Toby heard Mr. Bertram's ragged breathing sounding like a snore.

"No," Toby heard his father say. "Toby is a good boy. He don't smoke. You musta seen somebody else."

"I'm afraid not," Reverend Olsen said. "I'm afraid we've got a real problem on our hands, Mr. Thurston. And I feel awful. I feel that I'm totally to blame, letting it go so long. And it was so obvious. But it all fits together now. Where's Toby?" he asked.

"I don't know," Toby heard his father's quiet reply.

"Every time I come here and ask, you or your wife don't know. Well, that's not unusual, I always thought. He's off playing, like other kids. But now we know where Toby was all those times. He was in the church basement, smoking in the company of disgusting posters." Reverend Olsen cleared his throat. "I think Bertram here will support me in this: Toby needs help. The things he's doing are probably cries for help—and we weren't listening. Certainly he needs counseling. Probably a foster home." Toby heard a board squeak as Reverend Olsen shifted his weight. He pictured Reverend Olsen reaching out to put an arm around his father's shoulder and his father shrinking away. "I know it's hard, Thurston. But we must face facts. Toby needs help."

"Reverend Olsen, I want you off a my porch. Now." Toby's ears buzzed at the sound of his father's voice, so strong and so sure. "An' you too, Mr. Bertram. Toby is a good boy an' my son an' I love 'im. An' nobody's takin' 'im away."

"If you love him, listen to us," Reverend Olsen said evenly.

"Off my porch. Now. 'Fore I git the police."

"Git the police!" Mr. Bertram cried. "I got broke into! And *you* want to git the police!" The sagging boards above Toby threatened to splinter under Mr. Bertram's swaying, angry weight.

"Come, now, Bertram," Reverend Olsen's voice was soothing and low. "Let's go now. I'll see to this in the morning. You'll see. Let's leave this to those who can help Toby, not the police."

"Well I don't like it." Mr. Bertram spat and Toby flinched when it landed above him.

The porch shuddered and shook as Mr. Bertram and Reverend Olsen walked together toward the stairs.

"You ain't heard the last of me, Thurston!" Toby heard Mr. Bertram yell as he walked down the sidewalk. "While Toby's on the loose, I'll be a-waitin' fer 'im! I'll teach 'im a thing or two!"

Toby listened as his father shuffled inside and closed the screen door.

Toby wanted to rush into his father's arms and bury his face into his father's stomach. But like a wounded animal, Toby curled tighter and tried to draw further into himself. The front door closed.

12

Toby woke to the sound of glass splintering. He craned his neck to look toward the porch's opening and saw Whiskers's dark shape from the back. She was standing, her head low, her tail still. She growled softly and Toby heard a hollow thump and clatter as something hit the wooden siding on the front of the house and rolled back across the porch, coming to rest right above where he lay.

"Don't!" Toby heard someone outside. "Harold, I . . . insist!" The voice was Robin's.

Toby rolled onto his hands and knees and crawled toward the opening until he was shoulder to shoulder with Whiskers. He felt Whiskers taut and trembling as she sniffed, searching for smells.

Toby tensed as something else hit the house. "Harold!" Robin warned. Toby pushed past Whiskers and stuck his head out into the lilac-scented night air. "Shut up!" hissed another voice. The Bertrams' house was dark and silent. The lurking hulk of Mr. Bertram's car sat in the driveway like a hungry lion on its haunches pretending to sleep.

Toby searched the darkness for movement and sound. The restless night air washed coolness over his eyes and he blinked. He caught the movement of a bat, darting and zigzagging in the night sky as if trying to stitch the stars together and greeting each one with a high-pitched squeak.

The tops of the trees swayed gently in a puff of air and a dog barked in the distance. Suddenly a rock streaked toward the house, growing larger as it approached, like a meteor from space. Toby ducked his head as it hurtled overhead, shattering a window next to the front door. Glass rained onto the floor inside with a delicate tinkle and Toby scooted farther out into the lilac bushes on his chest, his head turned in the direction from which the rock came.

"Stop it!" Toby turned toward Robin's voice and saw a head disappear into a clump of bushes between the Bertrams' driveway and his house. Another head popped up from the other side of the clump and an arm whipped out and over it. Toby hugged the ground as a rock flew through the air and smacked the screen door and fell, rattling, to the porch.

"I'm . . . appalled *and* I'm leaving." Toby saw Robin's head rise above the bushes as she stood up. But a hand grabbed her arm and pulled her down. "Let go or I'll . . ."

Coming from inside the house, Toby heard the slap of feet trotting toward the door. A head popped out from the middle of the clump as a rectangle of light flashed on, spilling from the window and stretching over tufts of grass that looked like the tops of tousled heads in the night light. John, Toby observed, squinting at the head before it disappeared. He heard the front door open and the screen door hinges complain. A door-shaped patch of light spread over the sidewalk, bleaching the grass on either side.

"Wha' is goin' on?" Toby heard his father's voice, strained and frightened. Toby's father took a step and his foot hit a rock, skittering it across the porch. The rock bumped down the stairs and onto the sidewalk.

Toby watched as two heads popped up, first John's and then Harold's, from behind the clump of bushes. Arms flashed pale in the eerie light and Toby held his breath as two rocks pelted toward the porch. Toby cringed as one rock hit the side of the house solidly. And his stomach twisted painfully as the other rock hit its target with a dull thud.

"Ohh," he heard his father gasp. Boards groaned as his father staggered several steps. "Wha's goin' on here?"

he heard his father yell in a pain-soaked voice.

"Let go of me!" Robin grunted, standing up.

Toby scrambled to his feet, clawing the ground, his legs churning before he was upright. A lilac branch whipped across his face, burning, but his eyes didn't flinch from where Robin stood. Robin's head jerked in his direction and her eyes widened. Toby saw Pete's head poke above the bushes and his eyes widen and his mouth drop when he saw him coming.

Whiskers passed Toby and beat him around the bushes.

"Ow!" a startled voice yelled. "Ow!" The surprise turned to fear. Toby heard Whiskers growl as she spun around the bushes. Toby swerved to keep from tripping over Whiskers. "N-no-no-n-no," John stammered as he scrambled to get away from Whiskers. The dog leaned back on her haunches to brake herself, John's shirt clamped in her mouth and stretching with little warning rips. Toby saw Harold crawling frantically toward the street, his rear end stuck up like a stinkbug's. Harold looked back over his shoulder and Toby saw panic frozen in his face.

Toby's anger fed on Harold's panic and grew to a rage that spun in his head like a tornado. He leaped up and threw himself through the air, butting Harold's upended rear with the crown of his head. Harold crumped forward to the ground and Toby clawed his way toward Harold's head, grabbing hunks of cloth and skin and muscle.

He closed his eyes and beat blindly at Harold's head

and neck and shoulders as Harold twisted and turned under him like a fat lizard. Toby grunted with the effort of each punch, and Harold's cry was interrupted with breathless silence each time Toby hit between his shoulder blades. Toby's eyes flew open and his arms froze in midair as a strong hand grabbed his shoulder. He twisted his head to the right and looked up into Mr. Bertram's stubby face. He smelled bug juice on Mr. Bertram's breath.

Harold heaved himself up with his arms. Toby teetered and began to fall backward, but Mr. Bertram's hand steadied him. Toby hooked his feet under Harold's belly and pulled his legs tight. Harold collapsed again onto the ground.

"Well I'll be," Mr. Bertram said, pulling Pete onto his tippy toes by his shirt collar. Pete's helpless eyes were those of a kitten being carried in its mother's mouth by the scruff of its neck.

Harold made a weak attempt to get up from the ground. Mr. Bertram planted his foot on the base of Harold's neck and stepped down. "You better stay put if ya know what's good fer ya," he growled to Harold. He peered through the darkness at Robin. "Who the hell are you?" he asked, his eyes roaming up and down her body. They paused on her chest and slowly rose to meet her eyes.

Robin stared and hugged herself as if she were cold. She opened her mouth but no sound came out. She tried again. "I'm . . . Robin."

Toby got to his feet. His knees popped and felt weak

and his hands tingled from pounding on Harold. He looked down at the side of Harold's face, pressed against the ground, his eye wide open like a fish eye.

Toby looked past Robin to Whiskers. John's shirt had torn, releasing him. But Whiskers's tail was straight out and bristled. Her ears were drawn tight against her head, her teeth were bared, and her nose twitched inches from John's face. John was on his hands and knees, his eyes locked into a stare-down with Whiskers. Terrified, John's eyes bugged sideways, toward Toby. Whiskers growled and John's eyes snapped back to Whiskers, glinting tears.

Toby's father walked down the porch steps wearing only a baggy pair of white Jockey shorts and was peering down at his own bare feet, stepping gingerly. Toby noticed that he was rubbing himself as if he were polishing his bottom rib.

The light from the doorway dimmed as Toby's mother's shape punched a black shadow in the bright rectangle stretched over the sidewalk. "Wha's hoppinning?" she called. A night breeze pressed her nightgown into her shins.

"Don' know," Toby's father called up to her, pulling the elastic band of his underwear up over his belly button.

"C-c-could you g-g-get this dog-g-g away from m-m-me?" John stammered.

Toby looked back at John and Whiskers. They hadn't moved a fraction of an inch. "Come 'ere," Toby called to Whiskers, patting his thigh. Whiskers stuck her nose closer to John's face and growled. John yelped. His head didn't move, but the skin of his face pulled back toward his ears. Whiskers's lips flapped down over her teeth and she walked slowly to Toby.

"Don't jes' stand there lookin' ugly," Mr. Bertram barked at Toby's father. "Grab 'im 'fore he gits away."

Toby's father reached under John's armpit and pulled him to his feet. "He's the one threw that rock what hit 'cha." Mr. Bertram glared at John. "Saw 'im do it from ma house. Was a-waitin' up ta catch Toby, here, and was dozin' off when I heard the glass breakin' over your place. Looked out jes' in time an' next thing I know Toby tied into 'im like a wild thing." Mr. Bertram glared at Toby. "Don't know what's goin' on. But I don't like it."

Mr. Bertram motioned toward his house with his shoulder. "Since you don't have a phone, let's take these brats"—Mr. Bertram spat the word—"ta my house and give our ol' friend Olsen a call." He looked down at Harold. "Try anything funny, boy, and you'll be wishin' you was on a chain gang." He lifted his foot and kept it cocked upward and ready to strike as Harold slowly got to his feet.

Mr. Bertram grabbed Harold by his shirt collar and, a boy in each hand, marched toward his house. John stumbled alongside Toby and Toby's father and shrugged his shoulders to loosen Mr. Thurston's grip. Robin walked behind. "I'll b'back soon," Toby's father called over his shoulder. Toby looked back at his mother and saw her grab the door frame to steady herself and lift one hand as if to wave. She dabbed her eyes instead.

The Bertrams' front door flew open just as they mounted the stairs. Mrs. Bertram stepped out, her hair glowing white in the night-light.

"Ya caught 'em!" she chortled. "Ya caught them nasty little poltergeists." She looked from her son to Toby. "Knew you would catch 'em, little ghosty boy." She ran up and hugged Toby to her bony chest. She let go of Toby and danced a jig on the porch, laughing and chanting words over and over in a singsong: "Nasty little poltergeists. Nasty lit-tle poltergeists."

Mr. Bertram's face hardened as he looked back to his mother. "Momma, these the kids what broke in and took yer wireless and pennies?"

Mrs. Bertram cackled. "Not that'n." She pointed at Robin. "But that'n and that'n and that'n." She pointed at Harold and John and Pete. "An' now they gonna pay. Whoopee! Gonna pay. Gonna pay." She danced into the house, her green bathrobe flipping and flapping around her feet.

"Olsen?" Mr. Bertram bellowed into the phone. "You best be gittin' yer butt over here. We got ourselves a little problem." He listened, rolling a new cigar up and down the length of his mouth. "Toby? Ya. He's here. But let's stop yakkin' on the phone and you git over here. Hear?" And he slammed down the phone.

Mr. Bertram looked at Toby's father. "Thurston, ya look like a plucked chicken. An' they's ladies present."

He nodded toward Robin, who stood behind Toby's father.

Toby's father looked over his shoulder and saw Robin for the first time. He moved beside John to hide from her. "Toby," he said, quietly. "You go home an' find me somethin' ta wear?"

Mr. Bertram looked over to his mother. "Momma, go git Thurston a nightshirt or somethin', will ya?"

Mrs. Bertram scurried from the room and came back with a nightshirt that looked as if it were made from a whole sheet. A knocking came from the front door. As she headed for the door, she flung the nightshirt toward Toby's father and it flew through the air, hanging like a ghost.

Reverend Olsen walked in. His rumpled paisley pajama top was half tucked into his pants. A corner of paisley flannel stuck out of his half-zipped fly. His hair was mussed and he was wearing slippers.

Toby stared at Reverend Olsen. He'd never seen him before without his clerical collar. His neck looked long and skinny and pale. Reverend Olsen stared back at Toby, tired and cross, his eyes puffy with sleep. He turned toward Mr. Bertram and his eyes sprang awake at the sight of Harold and Pete. His jaw muscle pulsed as he worked the back of his mouth. "Harold, I thought you were in bed. What are you doing here at this hour of the night?"

Harold shrugged his shoulders and opened his mouth to say something.

"We didn't mean to hurt anybody," Pete blurted. All

heads snapped toward Pete. "We just wanted to . . . You tell him, Robin."

Reverend Olsen looked toward Robin and, surprised, his jaw stopped working.

Harold's face screwed into tight anger. "Shut up," he barked. His leg flashed out and struck Pete between the legs.

"Oh," Pete moaned, folding over to hug his crotch. Mr. Bertram grabbed Pete's shirt collar to keep Pete from falling on his head.

With his other hand, Mr. Bertram grabbed the scruff of Harold's shirt and shook. "Stop that," he growled. "What 'cha gotta say?" As he looked at Robin, his eyes bunched into unfriendly slits.

"We came to give back a . . ."

"She's a crazy lady," Harold interrupted. He looked at Mrs. Bertram and clenched his teeth to keep them from chattering. Looking at Robin he spat, "She doesn't know what she's talking about."

"Listen, you," Mr. Bertram snarled, lifting Harold from the ground. "I don't . . ."

Reverend Olsen rushed up to Mr. Bertram. "You let my son down this instant," he ordered. "I won't have you abusing my boy in this way."

Mr. Bertram slowly lowered Harold. "Olsen," he said, his cigar sticking straight out and almost touching Reverend Olsen's nose. "These kids was throwin' rocks at the Thurston house. Broke a coupl'a windows and that 'un"—he tipped his head toward John—"hit Thurston right in the breadbasket with one the size of my fist."

Mr. Bertram let go of Harold and waved a fist in Reverend Olsen's face. "Caught 'em red-handed. Now you tell me who's abusin' who."

A startled Reverend Olsen lowered his gaze to Harold. "Is that so?" he asked quietly.

"We were just trying to . . ." Harold said slowly, his eyes shifting back and forth, searching every corner of the room for a way out.

"It's all your fault!" Pete stood, his face red from bending over. His mouth quivered as he looked sideways at Harold, inching away in case Harold struck again. "You were the one who wanted to take that radio and those pennies. And you were the one who wanted to make everybody think Toby did it."

"Nobody made you do anything, you little bastard," John muttered, shrugging out of Mr. Thurston's hand and throwing himself on Pete. They fell to the floor and Toby's father lowered the nightshirt over John's head and shoulders like a net and jerked him off Pete. "Let go of me!" John's muffled voice came through the nightshirt. The cloth covering his mouth dented each time he breathed in.

Robin cleared her throat and stepped around John. Her hand trembled as she held it out to Mrs. Bertram.

"I wanted to leave this in your . . . car," she said. "I didn't know it was . . . stolen when Harold gave it to me. That's what I thought we were doing tonight," she said, fighting tears. "I didn't know that they wanted to . . . vandalize Toby's house."

Mrs. Bertram squinted at Robin's hand. "Cain't see

nothin'," she said, squinting up into Robin's face.

Robin's fingers uncurled and Mrs. Bertram looked back down. In Robin's palm was the brooch with ivy leaves surrounding a faded photograph of Mrs. Bertram. "Well, I'll be," Mrs. Bertram said, reaching out and picking it up. "Almost looks like me too," she said, looking around the faces surrounding her and smiling. "Look better now dead than when I was alive." She whooped and held it up for her son to see. "Lookee!"

Reverend Olsen looked from Mrs. Bertram to Harold, his mouth open. Red patches glowed on both cheeks, as if he'd been slapped. Harold stared defiantly back at his father. "Is this true?" his father whispered.

Harold clamped his mouth tighter and stared at his father. "Harold, answer me." Reverend Olsen's voice rose, spiraling, like a cry for help.

Still Harold only stared hatefully at his father.

"Harold!" Reverend Olsen raised his hand threateningly above his head. His fingers trembled and then they struck, leaving red stripes across the side of Harold's face.

Still Harold stared, more hateful than before.

"We made the hideout in the basement," Pete babbled. "And we put up posters. And we broke into the Bertrams'. And we were gonna take Toby's dog and make a rug out of her. And we were gonna . . ." Pete looked with bug eyes around the circle of faces surrounding him. His eyes stopped at Mrs. Bertram's. "I'm sorry," he said, biting his lower lip. His eyes filled and tears dripped from his nose. He snuffed them up. "I'm sorry," he said, turning to Toby.

Toby turned to Mr. Bertram. "Told'ja I didn't do it," he said, straightening his back and lifting his chin. He looked Mr. Bertram directly in the eye, surprised at his boldness.

Mr. Bertram took the cigar out of his mouth. He ran his tongue around his lips several times and scratched the top of his head. "That so," he said. He put the cigar back in his mouth. "I ain't so sure."

Reverend Olsen hadn't taken his eyes from Harold. "How could you do this to me?" he asked, pain stretching his voice. "How *dare* you do this to me?" His chin trembled. Harold's hateful stare flickered for just a moment and then renewed itself, more intense than before.

Toby felt a hand on his shoulder. His father leaned over and whispered in his ear, "Let's g'home, Toby."

Toby's mother greeted them at the door on tippy-toe, her arms open wide. Toby's father had draped Mr. Bertram's nightshirt over his shoulder like a large cape. He opened it and drew Toby and his wife into its folds. Whiskers sat on her haunches and looked up at them, her mouth open in a dog smile.

Together they cleaned up, Toby holding the dustpan as his father swept shards of glass into it. His mother tacked pillowcases and dishtowels over the broken windows. As Toby and Whiskers walked out back to the garbage cans with a paper sack full of broken glass, Toby looked over at the Bertrams' house. The kitchen light burned bright.

As Toby and Whiskers came through the kitchen, they heard the soft ebb and flow of his parents' voices in the living room. Toby flickered off the kitchen light as he entered the living room. His parents looked up at him from where they sat on the couch.

"Come 'ere, son," his father said, patting the cushion beside him.

Toby walked around the couch and sat next to his father. He leaned into his father's side and rested his head in the hollow under his father's arm. He breathed deeply of his father's familiar smell and felt safe.

"To-bee," his mother said, reaching across her husband and taking one of Toby's hands in her own. "We wan' to tall-ka-bout somethin' wi' you," she said loudly and slowly. Toby sat up and looked into his mother's face—pinched with the effort of talking clearly.

Toby studied his mother's face. His mother's clear blue eyes looked back at him, steady as a child's.

"We know yer a goo-d boy," his mother said, squeezing his hand. "An' we wan' the bes' for you. To-bee, we wan-der if you ma-bee should live wi' yer Gran'paw an' Gran'maw Thur-stone. Ma-bee we aren' good enough pair-ants fer you."

Toby looked from his mother to his father. He shook his head and looked down the length of his father's ropy leg. Between his father's knees he saw Whiskers, lying at his feet, looking at him, her ears pricked up and alert.

Toby looked shyly at his mother through his eyelashes. "I don't wanna go anyplace," he said. "You're my momma and my poppa." He looked at his father. "We can take care of each other."

His father's face relaxed with relief and the corners of his eyes crinkled up as a smile spread across his face. "You sure?" he asked.

Toby shrugged and then nodded. "I'll help more around the house. Maybe get me a job."

"To-bee, we proud of a you." His mother beamed at him from her side of the couch. "You jes' wor-ray 'bout bean a boy. We'll wor-ray 'bout mon-aie."

Toby reached over his father and met his mother as she leaned over to hug him.

"Woo-ah," Toby's father grunted playfully. Toby felt himself being lifted up and turned, like a baby, in the air so that he faced his smiling father. As relaxed and trusting as a baby, Toby dangled above his father's head. Slowly his father lowered him so that Toby sat on his lap facing him. His father's face was serious. "We got more love than brains in this fam-bly. But I'd a rather have love." He smiled shyly. "Toby, will ya teach me how ta do my figgers?" he asked.

Toby nodded and thought of Harold. *More brains than love. Maybe that's what makes Harold so mean.*

Toby threw himself against his father's chest. He

closed his eyes and hugged tight. He felt a love for his father and his mother that hurt inside—as though his heart were giving birth.

Toby was glad to be born and he cried with the pleasure of being alive. And being loved.

About the Author

Marc Talbert grew up in the plains states of the American West. After college he taught elementary school and soon began writing about the concerns of his young students. His first book was *Dead Birds Singing*, about which Jim Trelease, author of *The Read-Aloud Handbook*, wrote, "[It] is one of the most powerful books I've ever read. . . . I can still picture whole scenes from the book." A second novel, *Thin Ice*, has recently been published.

Mr. Talbert and his wife now live in Tesuque, near Santa Fe, New Mexico.